"Feel, *bella*. Feel how much you're exciting me." Xavier moved Trella's ha[nd] ... the sash, so ... slammed i... anything I'... either."

Her scalp tingled. She dropped her champagne, ignoring the delicate break of crystal, wanting too badly to touch him with both hands. She slid her fingers to the back of his neck and raised her mouth, inviting him to kiss her. It was pure instinct and he didn't hesitate, covering her parted lips as though he'd been let off his leash after being tempted too long.

The world stopped, then spun the other way, dizzying her. She made one whimpering noise, astonished by how thoroughly such a thing could devastate her, wilting all her muscles.

She distantly heard another delicate shatter, then he picked her up, lifting his head to reveal a fierce expression. Victory? Not quite, but there was something conquering there. Something exalted.

Yet his bright gaze asked a question.

She nodded, unable to speak, just gave herself up to it, to him. She knew when to fight her body and when to surrender. Perhaps it was the silver lining to all those years of having to accept that physiology trumped logic. This was bigger than anything she could make sense of.

## The Sauveterre Siblings

*Meet the world's most renowned family...*

Angelique, Henri, Ramon and Trella—two sets of twins born to a wealthy French tycoon and his Spanish aristocrat wife. Fame, notoriety and an excess of bodyguards are the prices of being part of their illustrious dynasty. And wherever the Sauveterre twins go, scandal is sure to follow!

They're protected by the best security money can buy, and no one can break through their barriers... But what happens when each of these Sauveterre siblings meets the one person who can breach their hearts?

Meet the heirs to the Sauveterre fortune in Dani Collins's fabulous quartet:

*Pursued by the Desert Prince*

*His Mistress with Two Secrets*

*Bound by the Millionaire's Ring*

*Prince's Son of Scandal*

Available now!

# Dani Collins

—

# PRINCE'S SON OF SCANDAL

ISBN-13: 978-1-335-50399-2

Prince's Son of Scandal

First North American publication 2017

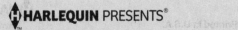

**HARLEQUIN** PRESENTS®

Recycling programs
for this product may
not exist in your area.

ISBN-13: 978-1-335-50399-2

Prince's Son of Scandal

First North American publication 2017

Copyright © 2017 by Dani Collins

Printed in U.S.A.

www.Harlequin.com

Canadian **Dani Collins** knew in high school that she wanted to write romance for a living. Twenty-five years later, after marrying her high school sweetheart, having two kids with him, working at several generic office jobs and submitting countless manuscripts, she got The Call. Her first Harlequin novel won the Reviewers' Choice Award for Best First in Series from *RT Book Reviews*. She now works in her own office, writing romance.

## Books by Dani Collins

### Harlequin Presents

*The Secret Beneath the Veil*
*Bought by Her Italian Boss*
*Vows of Revenge*
*Seduced into the Greek's World*
*The Russian's Acquisition*

### The Sauveterre Siblings

*Pursued by the Desert Prince*
*His Mistress with Two Secrets*
*Bound by the Millionaire's Ring*

### The Secret Billionaires

*Xenakis's Convenient Bride*

### The Wrong Heirs

*The Marriage He Must Keep*
*The Consequence He Must Claim*

### Seven Sexy Sins

*The Sheikh's Sinful Seduction*

Visit the Author Profile page
at Harlequin.com for more titles.

Back in 2012, I received a call—*the call*—from editor Megan Haslam, telling me she wanted to buy my book. It was my first sale and terribly exciting. I have since worked with some of the other fabulous editors in the London office, but with *Prince's Son of Scandal*, I came back to working with Megan. I'd gone so far down a rabbit hole with Trella in the first three books of this quartet, I really wasn't sure I could pull off her story. Megan offered just the right feedback to help me make it work. We're reunited and it feels so good!

I'd also like to dedicate this book to you, dear reader, for your wonderful letters and support for The Sauveterre Siblings. I'm so glad you love these characters as much as I do. xo

# CHAPTER ONE

*Six months ago...*

WHEN THE GREETER at the ballroom entrance asked Trella Sauveterre for her name, she nearly gave an arrogant "you know who I am."

She bit it back. Her sister was never acerbic. Not with strangers, and definitely not with underlings. Her twin was perfectly capable of terse words and might even hurl some blue ones at Trella when she learned what she was doing right now, but Angelique's personality was one of sensitivity and empathy. Gentleness and kindness.

Trella? Not so much.

"Angelique Sauveterre," Trella lied, wearing her sister's polite yet reserved smile. She ought to feel more guilty. She ought to feel like an overused cliché from a children's movie, but she didn't.

She felt *alive*.

And apprehensive. Terror could overcome her

if she let herself dig deep enough. This was like swimming toward the middle of a lake, where the bottom was too deep to imagine. Who knew what dangers lurked in those dark watery depths? Monsters. They existed. She had met them. Had nearly been consumed by them.

But she wouldn't think about that.

Nothing in her outward appearance revealed the way her heart bounced and jostled in her chest, fighting internal battles. She moved gracefully, even though her muscles felt stiff and petrified, twitching to run.

Because, along with the trickles of fear, a tumbling waterfall of joy rang through her. It was all she could do to keep tears from her eyes or laughter from escaping her throat.

*I'm doing it!* she wanted to call her family and cry. *Look. I'm in public. By myself. I'm not shriveling like a vampire in the sun.*

But they didn't know where she was and it was best to keep it that way. This was the sort of sneaking out a window she should have done years ago, when she'd been an adolescent. Instead, she'd been a grieving survivor with an eating disorder and more baggage than a passenger jet.

Still was, if these people only knew.

She quashed the negative self-talk and moved like a normal person through the crowd. Gazes lingered, noting Angelique Sauveterre had arrived. Her bodyguard kept anyone from approaching, though. Maybe that wasn't normal for everyone, but it was for the Sauveterre twins, even the eldest set of brothers.

With her sister's aloof nod, she returned a few greetings to people she imagined she was supposed to know.

In a few weeks, she would come out as Trella and have nothing left to hide behind. No more walls, literal or technical. No broad-shouldered brothers. No playing her sister to avoid being herself. She had determined, had sworn on the blood she had shed when she nicked her ear cutting her own hair before Christmas, that this was the year she would free herself from the prison she had created.

For now, she was still hiding behind Angelique. She had impersonated her sister a few times recently, with her sister's permission, escorted by their brother Henri to watch his twin, Ramon, race. They'd also taken in a fellow designer's latest collection during fashion week. It had been spectator stuff where they didn't interact with anyone and kept to places her sister had been seen with their brothers before.

Trella had never walked out in public alone. In her entire life, she had rarely done anything alone. As a child, Angelique—Gili to her family—had been the needy one and Trella, the protector. She had held Gili's hand so her sister wouldn't tremble and cry at the attention they had received. Their brothers had barely given them breathing space even before Trella's kidnapping at age nine, always ready to catch a tumble from a swing or to keep them from wandering too far from the group.

Then she'd been stolen and had *wished* that her captors had left her alone.

She swallowed and veered her mind away from those memories. They were guaranteed to bring on an attack and she was doing far too well. It was coming up to two years without one.

The attacks had manifested years after her rescue, when she should have been finding her feet and moving on with her life. Instead, she had become a horrible burden. Her siblings would never say so, but they had to be sick of being on call for her. She was certainly tired of being the weakest link. She *had* to change.

Tonight was another step toward that. The press would go mad when she finally came out of seclusion at a friend's wedding in a few weeks. She had to be ready, but she had to *know* she was ready.

So she was testing herself, if somewhat impulsively, because this charity dinner hadn't been on her agenda at all when she had arrived in Paris.

She had been beside herself with pride when she'd landed, high on travelling from the family home in Spain—by private jet with trusted guards, always—but without her mother or siblings. It had taken her newfound independence to the next level.

So, when Gili tentatively had asked if she could run to London for a hot secret weekend with her new paramour, *of course* Trella had told her to go. Her sister had looked incandescent when she'd spoken about Prince Kasim. He was clearly something special.

Trella wanted her sister to be happy, wanted to quit holding her back. Spending a night alone at their tightly secured living space above their design house, Maison des Jumeaux, had seemed a perfect cherry on top of Trella's already sweet split from old fears.

As the evening stretched on, however, she had restlessly poked around the flat, picking up after her sister and teetering on feeling sorry for herself. Wistfulness had closed around her.

Would *she* ever have a romantic liaison? Her feelings about men were so ambivalent. At fourteen, she'd had the usual rush of hormonal interest, even shared an embrace with the gardener's son behind a rosebush. Then their father had died and the most terrifying predators had emerged online, threatening her in vile ways. Her fear of men, of *everything*, had compounded a hundred-fold. As her panic attacks escalated, the deep-est fear of all had crept into her very soul—that she was so damaged and broken, no one would ever want her.

For years, she had barely allowed men near her, interesting or otherwise. She slipped from one secured location to another through shielded walkways, accompanied by a mostly female guard detail. Occasionally, her brothers intro-duced her to a friend, but even if she had wanted any of those bankers or race-car drivers to make a pass, Ramon and Henri wouldn't have allowed it.

Their dearest family friend, Sadiq, was the only man she'd spent real time with and theirs had never been a romantic relationship. He was the shy, heart-of-gold computer nerd who had helped the police locate her, returning her to her family. She loved him, but as her savior, not as a man.

Which was why his engagement had shaken her out of her ivory tower. She would do any-thing for Sadiq. If he wanted her at his wed-ding, of course she would attend, even though it meant overcoming her demons and returning to the public eye.

It had been a struggle to come this far, but now, as she stood on the cusp of achieving something like a normal life, she found herself resetting the goalposts.

She wanted her sister's anticipation for a weekend with a man. She wanted to be the person she would have been if she hadn't been stolen and assaulted, stalked and bullied, but it would never happen if she kept living behind these damned walls!

A disgusted toss of the latest fashion magazines onto the coffee table had sent a pile of paperwork sliding to the floor, revealing an invitation to this ball.

The fundraiser benefited orphaned children, something that would go straight to Gili's tender heart. Even if Gili had sent regrets, the Sauveterre checkbook was always welcome.

Not letting herself overthink it, Trella had briefed a security team and slipped on one of her sister's creations.

Where Trella loved powerful touches like strong shoulders and A-lines, along with eye-catching beadwork and bold colors, her sister's style was gentler. The champagne gown had a waifish quality in the way the sleeves fell off her shoulders. The bodice and torso were fitted to her figure, but the ruched skirt across her hips created a sensual impression of gathered satin sheets around a nude form.

She added her sister's earrings and a locket

with a panic button, but kept the look simple, arranging her hair into a fall of dark locks and painting her lips a soft pink.

Now she was here, breathless and petrified, yet filled with more optimism than she'd experienced in years. She moved to speak to the aloof Russian host and his much warmer British wife, Aleksy and Clair Dmitriev.

"I'm so glad you came," Clair said, drawing her aside in a confiding way that revealed Clair had no idea she was talking to Gili's twin. "You're not my only supporter who comes without a date, but you're the only one who won't be silly about my guest of honor. Don't even ask how I got him here. I was hideously shameless, interrupting their trade talks and putting him on the spot in front of everyone. I talked him into auctioning himself for the first dance."

Trella scanned for a glimpse of this exalted personality. Clair continued her confession as she wound them through the crowd.

"Aleksy said at least I use my power for good instead of evil, but I feel a little evil because the ravens surrounded him the minute he arrived. They'll back off if you're there, though. I know you'll put him at ease. Everyone loves you. Do you mind?"

Trella could see how Clair got what she wanted, sounding sincere in her flattery as she took agreement for granted. Still, she was curious enough to murmur, *"Bien sûr,"* in her sister's preferred French.

Clair beamed and gently pushed into the thicket of gowns.

The mystery man turned, revealing a red sash beneath his black tuxedo jacket. He was tall. Intimidatingly tall, with broad shoulders and an economy of movement, suggesting a huntsman's physique lurked beneath his sophisticated attire. The blond glints in his light brown hair looked natural, given the hint of gold in his eyebrows.

*Those eyes.* They were such a piercing blue they struck like slabs off a glacier, peeling away to fall and rock the world. The rest of his features were precisely carved in sweeps of long cheeks under sharp cheekbones, a jaw hammered square and a mouth of two perfectly symmetrical peaks over a full but uncompromising bottom lip.

He was so compelling a force, so beyond her experience, the room faded from her consciousness. They became trapped in a noiseless, airless bubble as they took each other in.

Had she really longed to be seen as a woman? Because it was happening. He skimmed his gaze down in unabashed assessment. She saw the flash of interest in his gaze as it came back and locked with hers. He liked what he saw.

He saw Gili, though. Sweet Gili who was used to being in public, where men routinely sized her up as a potential conquest.

The strangest reaction slithered through Trella. She ought to have prickled with threat, or acted like Gili and let his male interest drift past her as if she didn't notice or care.

Instead, she took issue with her sister being seen as a trophy. Protective instincts honed since birth pushed her confrontational personality to the forefront of the image she presented.

*You'll have to go through me*, she projected, tucking Gili safely behind her.

His stare intensified. *Burned*. He saw *her*. Whatever shields she had walked in here holding—including her sister's persona—were gone. She felt completely unprotected against his thorough exploration of her face, his gaze touching each curve and dip of her features.

It felt like a spill of magic, making her cheeks tingle. She had to disguise a rush of unprecedented sensual awareness. Men didn't affect her, but the spell he cast sent invisible sensations from her throat to her nipples and her pelvis, into her thighs and terminated in a paralysis that nailed her feet to the floor. All the while, delicious stirrings swirled upward through her, making her feel drawn toward him.

"Your Highness," she heard Clair say from what seemed like another universe. "Have you met Angelique Sauveterre?"

"Ms. Sauveterre, the Crown Prince of Elazar, Xavier Deunoro."

Xavier had known exactly what he was doing when Clair Dmitriev had cornered him into making an appearance at her charity event. He was buying a future favor from her powerful husband, a man who was notoriously difficult to influence.

He had also known it would be an evening rife with what he had before him: Women in daring gowns, swishing their hips in enticement, sweeping lashes in false shyness while they twisted their hair in invitation.

As Europe's most eligible bachelor, he was used to having his pick from such an array. He only needed to drop a claw and let it pick up one of the brightly colored toys before him. It didn't matter which one fell into his hands. They were all the same, providing brief entertainment and something soft to embrace for a night, before forgetting them in the hotel room when he left the next morning.

Given the news he had received this morning, tonight's plaything would be his last before his royal duty took precedence. It was another reason he had agreed to this ridiculousness. At least he had a decent selection for his final visit to the amusement park.

He was taking his time singling out his companion. They all had their charms. Was he in the mood for voluptuous or fair? Should he be practical and choose the one wearing enough gold not to covet his own? Or go with the one who promised some spark as she set her chin and glared at the rest?

Then his hostess presented a newcomer like a gift, one who made the rest of the women take sharp little breaths and step back.

She was taller than most, with divine features that matched her name. Her skin was soft and flushed, too warm to be called cream yet not dark enough to be olive. Golden as a sunrise glancing off a snowy peak.

A muse, clearly, since he felt poetic stirrings just by gazing at her. How could he not admire her? Her figure was goddess-perfect, her mouth sinful, her eyes fey and mysterious, colored somewhere between gray and green. If he pulled her from the cloud of perfume surrounding them, he bet she would smell like mossy forest and clean cold streams.

That was what she presented on the surface, at least. In a blink, she had shifted ever so slightly and it was as if she'd hit exactly the right angle to catch and reflect the sun. Something less tangible than external beauty seemed to concentrate and strike out in a sharp white light that pierced his eyes, like a star being born.

She was the diamond in a bowl of imitations, a woman of facets and contrasts, infinitely fascinating and priceless. If recognizing that caused him a stab of regret because he didn't have time to fully explore her depths and contradictions, he ignored it. Such was his life. He took what he could, when he could.

Tonight, he would take her, *grazie mille*.

"Good evening." He bowed over her hand, letting his breath warm her knuckles and feeling the tiny flex of her reaction. "It's an honor to meet you."

"A rare treat indeed." The tilt of her lips suggested an inside joke. "The honor is mine."

"I've seated you at the VIP table," Clair said. "Please find your way when you're ready. Has everyone seen the silent auction items?" Clair broke up the knot of disgruntled women, most of whom drifted off.

A few opportunists remained, one being the redhead with the determined chin. He sighed inwardly as the redhead flashed a too sweet smile before asking, "Angelique, how is your sister? Still keeping to herself?"

Ah yes. That's why the name had struck him as familiar. The family had a tragic history. One

of the twin girls had been kidnapped as a child.
She was rumored to be batty, so they kept her
out of sight. As someone who had been reported
as everything from born of an alien to outright
dead, he put little store in such gossip, but did
wonder how she would respond to such a blatant intrusion. It was clearly meant to disconcert.

She swung a scythe-sharp glance at the redhead, revealing the compressed carbon beneath
her sparkle.

"She's excellent." Her tone struck him as
ironic. "What's your name? I'll tell her you were
asking about her."

"Oh." The redhead was startled, but flicked
him a glance and decided to take a final stab at
snaring his interest. "*Lady* Wanda Graves."

"I'll be sure you're added to our list." She
smiled distantly and turned to him. "Shall we
find our seats?"

She didn't see the redhead brighten briefly
before a darker thought struck, one that tightened her mouth. The other women who'd been
standing by widened their eyes then averted their
gazes before they scurried off.

He offered his arm and dipped his mouth to
her ear. "You have a blacklist?"

"Nosy people do not wear our label."

Catty, ruthless, or both? Either way, he was
entertained.

And now he was reminded that the sisters had some kind of design house. Women's fashion was last on his list of interests, but he took a fresh assessment of her gown, appreciating the peek of thigh exposed by the slit and the gather of strapless satin that left an expanse of upper chest and breast swell to admire.

"This is one of your creations? It's pure artistry."

"I can tell when I'm being patronized," she warned.

"Then you'll know I'm sincere when I say the dress is lovely, but I see the woman inside it. Which is the point, is it not?"

"Do you?" She tilted a considering look up at him, something dancing in the elfin green of her eyes. He could have sworn they were gray a minute ago. Her gaze dropped to his chest, where the band of silk slashed across his heart. "I see the crown, not the man. Which is what this is meant to convey, isn't it?"

Astute, but a woman who made her living with clothing would understand such nuances.

The sash in question felt unaccountably restrictive this evening. Duty hovered in his periphery, set there by a brief news item passed along from his PA about Bonnafete, a small principality in the Mediterranean. The reigning prince's daughter, Patrizia, had called off her marriage to an American real estate mogul.

Patrizia was a longtime acquaintance. Xavier was not as sorry as he had implied when he had sent his condolences. He was in need of a titled wife. His grandmother wanted him married so she could step down. Patrizia was infinitely suitable.

He had asked that his grandmother be made aware of the broken engagement. It was an acknowledgement of his responsibility toward her, their bloodline and the crown. Loath as he was to marry, he preferred to spearhead such actions himself, rather than wait for her to issue orders. She might be the one person on this earth with the power to govern his actions, but he didn't have to encourage it. He was confident she would approve and God knew she would let him know if she didn't.

"Is it heavy?" his final sown oat asked of his sash. The levelness in her tone told him she didn't mean physically, proving she was even more perceptive than he'd imagined.

Compassion was not something he looked for in anyone, though, least of all his temporary companions. There was no room for any weakness in his life. No one saw him flinch. No one was privy to his bitterness at the hand life had dealt him.

It was a wasted emotion to feel.

So he ignored the chance she might understand him in a way no one else ever had and held her chair. "Nothing could weigh me down while I'm in your beguiling company, *bella*."

She froze and looked over her shoulder. "Why did you call me that?"

"It's an endearment. Elazar's official language is an Italian dialect, though French and German are commonly spoken along with English." He adjusted her chair as she sank into it then leaned down to speak against her hair where it fell in loose waves against her nape. "Why? Don't you like it?"

Tiny bumps lifted on her skin in a shiver of reaction. Her nipples tightened into peaks against the silk that draped over them, making him smile. She liked it.

Awash in more sexual anticipation than he'd felt in a while, perhaps ever, he seated himself, pleased he would end his bachelorhood with such a terrific bang.

Trella was a natural extrovert. The chatter and color around her, the voices and music and attention, was like standing in the sunshine after years in an *oubliette*.

But to have this man glance at her with that admiring look on his face as he seated himself next to her was a deliciously sweet accompaniment. He was clearly an accomplished seducer,

wearing charm and entitlement as comfortably
as his sash, but she was excited to be singled out
by him all the same. It was the flirtation she had
yearned for.

"What brings you to Paris?" he asked.

Although, if she was going to do this, she
wasn't settling for plain vanilla.

"Surely you can do better than asking what a
nice girl like me is doing in a place like this?"

"Let me consult my app." He glanced at an
imaginary phone. "How about… What sign are
you?" He affected sincere interest.

Her mouth twitched. "Gemini. Twins. Obviously. You?"

"No idea. August sixth."

"Leo. The lion. King of the jungle."

"Obviously," he said, with a self-deprecating
tilt of the corner of his mouth.

She bit back a smile, intrigued by his position,
but only because she knew what it was to be in
the spotlight. He'd glossed over her query about
the weight of his crown, but surely he wearied
of attention and responsibility.

"You take horoscopes seriously?" he asked,
nodding at a server who offered them champagne.

"Not as a belief system, but I used it as inspi-
ration for a collection a few years ago. We used
it," she amended quickly, clearing her throat over

the white lie and sliding her gaze to ensure the people searching for their seats hadn't overheard her. It was well known in fashion circles that *Trella* had designed that particular line.

"How?" He seemed genuinely curious. "The patterns in the fabric?"

"Not that literal. More how the nature of each sign is perceived. They fall into different qualities, like fixed or mutable, and elements, like air and fire. There's a lot to play with. I work better with deadlines so I approached one sign a month. It was an interesting exercise." She leaned closer, wrinkling her nose. "Also a terrific marketing hook."

The corners of his mouth deepened. "Beauty *and* brains. Always an irresistible combination."

This prince, causing her heart to thud-thud under a simple compliment, should have sent her running. She had learned healthy caution from her childhood, but even though most men put her on edge, this one filled her with a giddy *lack* of fear. It was like breaking out of a shell. Like discovering she had the ability to fly.

She definitely wanted more time with him before this evening ended.

On impulse, she motioned for her guard, who was actually one of Gili's, and quietly gave him an instruction about the silent auction. He melted away.

Was she being too forward? Reckless?

Their table filled up, forcing her to wait to find out. Dinner passed in a blur of neutral conversation. Someone asked the Prince about his country's foray into green energy. She vaguely recalled his mountain kingdom between Italy and Austria had been accused of providing a tax haven during the world wars. Elazar sounded very modern and self-sufficient now. He spoke about exporting hydropower, since rivers and streams were one of their few natural resources. There was also a decade of investing in education, attracting engineering and technology start-ups, solar and wind power.

Her inner businesswoman should have been taking mental notes, but she was mesmerized by his casual command over his audience and subtly seduced with how close his sleeve came to touching her arm. Beneath the table, she imagined she could feel the heat from his thigh mere inches from her own. All she could think about was dancing with him.

*Dancing.* Tears pressed the backs of her eyes. She ached for that simple pleasure.

This adolescent reaction was ridiculous, but she let it happen. Embraced it. This is what she should have been doing at twenty, not hand-sewing sequins on mini-dresses for other young women to wear to exclusive clubs, killing hours with concentrated work so she could get through one day, one more hour, without a breakdown or the drugs that were supposed to prevent them.

Then Prince Xavier turned his terrifically handsome face toward her, bathing her in the light of his regard. "You must travel a great deal for your work? What drew you to fashion?"

He had given each of the others a moment in his attentive sunlight. Now it was her turn. He must engage in small talk with a thousand people a day, at ribbon cuttings and children's hospitals, but she would have sworn on her life the tension around his eyes eased as he met her gaze. He'd been doing his duty, impatiently waiting to get back to her. She felt delirious even as she prevaricated her way through her reply.

"Both of us are quite creative." Gili more so. She was the artist who designed out of love and ran the business out of necessity. Trella was the ambitious one, determined to turn a healthy profit. Practicality, not passion, had driven her into making her own clothes, because she couldn't bear being judged by trolls for merely *buying* something, let alone how it looked on her.

"We had some start-up help from our brothers but surprised them and ourselves with our success." Another fib. She wouldn't have rested until they were making buckets of money. She was competitive and driven by an I'll-show-you desire for revenge against those who had thrown shade.

"It can't be an easy field. I'm sure your success is due to hard work as much as anything else."

He was trying to get her into bed. She knew that with the brains he'd said he admired, but his flattery *worked*. She was ridiculously affected by his compliment. She wanted to say "It was a ton of work. Thank you for noticing." Gili was the face of Maison des Jumeaux, which meant she received the bulk of the credit—not that she didn't deserve a lot, but Trella worked just as hard and was not a naturally humble person. Hearing his praise went into her like a transfusion, tipping her further under his spell.

Their hostess moved to the podium to make a short speech, thanked the guests for their donations then announced the winners for the auction items. Trella grew increasingly self-conscious as the moments ticked down, certain she had truly lost her mind this time. Maybe she should leave before—

"Finally, our most coveted prize, a dance with the Prince of Elazar, has been won by… Angelique Sauveterre!"

The applause was polite, the knives in her back proverbial, but she felt them. She privately smirked, then blushed as Xavier showed no surprise. Was he so sure of her?

"I'm flattered."

"You should be. I promised to double the next highest bid. You had better dance well enough to be worth it."

"I do," he assured her, rising to help with her chair, doing that erotic thing of speaking against her hair so tingles raced all over her skin. "For that sort of generosity, *bella*, I'll give you the whole night."

Oh, he was good. Lightheadedness accosted her every time he called her *bella*, the same nickname her family called her. Her pulse pounded so hard she thought it would bruise her throat, but it fed the thrilling excitement washing over her. He made her feel so alluring. *Sexy.*

He made her feel as though he wanted *her.*

That was beyond captivating. She had spent a lot of dark nights telling herself how flawed she was, how she didn't want men anyway, so she didn't care if they didn't want her. She did want, though. She wanted to feel normal and alive. Happy and desirable.

The touch of his hand on the small of her back had a terrific effect on her. The awareness that had been teasing her all evening became a suffusion of deeply sensual lethargy. Dear Lord, was she becoming *aroused*?

It was what she'd envied her sister for—which was when it struck her what was happening. She and Gili had a twin connection. They didn't read each other's thoughts or anything so intrusive, but they picked up hints of the other's emotions despite whatever physical distance might separate them. The preternatural sense was stronger on Gili's side. Trella had been so messed up for years, taking anti-depressants to quash anxiety attacks, she hadn't been as receptive to her sister's moods.

Lately, however, she'd become more aware, particularly if Gili was restless or having an off day. Tonight, her sister was with a man who truly excited her. She was usually so careful, so rarely selfish, yet she was basking in something that made her incredibly happy.

Her sister's buoyant heart lightened Trella's. She was happy for Gili, happy her sister wasn't weighed down by all the things Trella had put her through. It added another lift of carefree joy to her own evening.

"You dance well yourself," Xavier said as he spun her in a waltz.

She was too exhilarated to respond. The sparkling ballroom circled around her in a kaleidoscope of colors. His embrace was confident and reassuring, making her feel light as a fairy.

"I feel like Cinderella." It was too true. She was the smudged sister who had escaped from the attic, wearing borrowed clothing to dance with a prince.

"You look like something out of a fairy tale." The line of his brow twitched and the corner of his mouth deepened, like he both surprised and disparaged himself for saying. "You're very beautiful," he added gruffly.

Gili was the beautiful one. Trella had fought hard to get back to the same weight as her sister, wanting to feel as good as Gili looked. She had let her hair grow out to her sister's length so she could impersonate her for her dry runs going out in public, but she never thought of herself as beautiful. She too often thought of herself as broken.

Not tonight. She diverted herself away from any thoughts other than how *glorious* this was. Around and around they went. His thighs brushed hers, his fingers splayed as though trying to touch more of her. She let her fingers trail closer to his collar so she could rest the side of one finger on the hot skin of his neck. It was electrifying. The magnetic sensations grew as he kept her dancing into the second song, tugging her toward an unknown crescendo. When someone tried to cut in, Xavier shrugged him off.

"The privilege of position?" she teased.

"I've never seen anyone glow like you. I'm enthralled." Again, misgiving seemed to flicker like a shadow across his face. He didn't like admitting to whatever he was feeling, but it added to her own exuberance.

"I feel like… I can't even describe it. Like it's Christmas. Like anything is possible." She brought her gaze down from the chandelier into the turquoise blue of his eyes.

She reminded herself that becoming over-excited could have a rebound effect. She didn't want to backslide. It would be a long fall from this height.

Then she forgot any sense of caution when he said, "I need to kiss you." The desire in his words was a sensual squeeze that stole her breath.

A very long time ago, she had been quick to agree to anything that sounded adventurous. A dungeon full of shackles and bars had kept her grounded since then, but somehow, with a few words, this man reached past all the darkness and invited her into the light. To be the impulsive, audacious person she was in her heart.

"Me, too," she said through sensitized lips. *It's only a kiss.*

His sharp gaze moved beyond her. The next thing she knew, he had her off the dance floor, through a small break in the crowd and into an alcove hidden by the giant fronds of a potted plant.

She wasn't given time to decide whether she'd been too quick to agree. His arm tightened across the small of her back, pulling her in, arching her against the layers of his tuxedo.

He was steely beneath his civilized covering. He knew what he wanted. His hot mouth covered hers without hesitation.

For a second, she was terrified. Not of him, but of how she would react. Would she panic?

Then her senses took in the way his mouth fit against hers, moving to part her lips, questing for her response. Something primitive moved in her, shaking her foundations, waking the woman she might have been if her life had been different, drawing her beyond old traumas into a place she barely understood.

Pleasure flooded her, making her stiffen, wary of such a strong reaction, but primal need quickly took over. Her brain might not be able to process what was going on, but her body knew how to respond.

Rather than put the brakes on, her hands went behind his neck. She found herself running her fingers into his short hair, shaping the back of his head as she drew herself up, parting her lips so he could plunder at will.

His arms tightened around her and she thought he made a growling noise. It should have scared her. Male aggression, especially the sexual kind, was something she'd taken pains to avoid.

Strangely, with excitement pulsing through her, she found herself thrilled by his response.

She kissed him back with abandon, just as if she knew what she was doing.

Something flashed behind her closed eyes and he abruptly lifted his head.

"That was a camera," he muttered, fingers digging in near her tailbone as he pressed her close enough to feel the thick shape straining the front of his trousers. "Let's find some privacy."

Her analytical mind urged caution, but her old self, her true self, trusted her instincts. She released a breathy, "Let's."

# CHAPTER TWO

HE DIPPED HIS head to lightly scrape his teeth against her neck, urging against her ear, "You leave first. I'll follow you upstairs."

She gasped, mind going blank before a million thoughts rushed in.

"You have a room here? In the hotel?" What had she thought when he had said *privacy*? Was the idea of being alone with him intriguing or alarming?

"The penthouse, yes."

"Is it safe?"

"Of course." Good gracious he was handsome, even when he frowned. His features weren't too refined. There was just enough toughness in the intensity of his gaze, just enough stubbornness in the square of his jaw to make him look stern and rugged.

As he read her hesitation, his hand cupped the side of her head while his gaze flicked with irritation at the noise around them. "I want you to myself."

Empathy panged within her. She knew the wear and tear that being in the spotlight took on a person. She instantly wanted to give him the break he needed. He was a sophisticated man. She had nothing to fear from him physically, but was compelled to say, "I have guards. For a reason."

She was using her sister's tonight, both to give her own a much-deserved night off as well as to maintain the illusion she was her twin. *She should tell him who she was.*

"The room is completely secure. More secure than here," he added, mouth twisting in dismay at their having been photographed. He led her back to their table. "I won't keep you waiting long."

Voices of caution crowded into her head, but when would she have a free pass like this again? When would she meet a man who made her feel anything like this? It wasn't just physical, although that part was so heady she felt drunk, but there was a rarity, too. There were other men in the world who were a safe bet, men vetted by her brothers, but when would she feel this pull? This compulsion to know more about *this* man?

Before she talked herself out of it, she let her finger press *up* for the penthouse. It wasn't that she didn't have misgivings, or that she ignored them, she *overcame* them. It was different. It was another small triumph that had her stepping lightly off the elevator onto thickly carpeted floor.

It was easy to spot the Prince's room. Two guards were stationed outside the door. Her own accompanied her as she approached them.

"Mademoiselle Sauveterre," one greeted with a respectful nod. "We were notified to expect you." He stepped inside and invited her guard to sweep the rooms.

Both men behaved with the utmost professionalism, not betraying a hint of judgment about what they must know was a preliminary for seduction.

A smile touched her mouth as she thought about how her brothers would blow their tops if they knew where she was right now, even though they had both been on the Prince's side of this equation hundreds of times, the hypocrites.

Then she was left alone and she took in the elegant shades of ivory and sage green on the walls and the furnishings. A glass of watered-down Scotch had been abandoned on an end table, ice long melted. She sniffed, then dared a sip, thought about looking at the view, then decided to leave the drapes closed.

The double doors to the bedroom stood open. She stared at the bed, taking another quick sip of liquid courage just as the main door opened.

His star power impacted her anew, making her heart skip.

"You made yourself comfortable. Good."

"This is yours." She tilted the glass, then set it aside, instantly wishing she'd kept it to keep her hands busy.

"I'll make you a fresh one. Or, how about champagne?" He moved to the bar. As he peeled the foil from a bottle, the crinkle seemed overly loud.

This was the moment she should have admitted she was Trella.

A very real fear sat within that admission— that he would develop his own misgivings. He would either want explanations she didn't care to give, or he might jump to conclusions that made him averse to being with her. In no scenario did she imagine this exciting, lighthearted atmosphere would continue.

"You're nervous," he noted as he popped the cork.

"You're observant," she said, compelled to at least confess, "I don't do this."

It was true no matter which twin she represented. Gili running away for a weekend with a prince was as out of character as her being here with this one.

"I already guessed that." He set two glasses as he poured, canting his head to eye her. "You're not a virgin, are you?"

She choked. "No."

True again for both twins, but she had to look away, mind skipping off the dark memory like a stone off the water's surface.

No, that was another reason she was here. Being alone with a man was another snapped link in the chain that bound her to the past. She was really, really proud of herself right now. Even though her proffered excuse of "I'm just out of my comfort zone" was the understatement of the year.

He brought the glasses across the room to her and offered her one. *"Saluti."*

*"Salud."*

They sipped, gazes locked, unspoken expectations hovering between them. Her throat grew abraded by the bubbles.

"What if I change my mind about being here?" she asked in a soft rasp.

"Then I will be disappointed." His intent expression didn't change.

"Angry?"

"Disappointed. Very disappointed, *bella.*" His gaze acted like wildfire, igniting her blood as he swept it across her cheek and down her throat.

He turned away to set music playing. The notes were low and sultry, matching the thick feeling in her veins, the sensual throb of her pulse.

"Either way, I'm pleased to have you to myself." He came back to her, steps laconic, touch smooth and confident as he looped his arm around her. "Whether you want to talk or dance or…pass the time in other ways."

He swayed them into a dance that was really just the press of two bodies. Foreplay. They both still held their champagne flutes. Held gazes.

"I wasn't in the mood to fight other men for your attention."

"Was anyone else even trying? I hadn't noticed." She batted her lashes.

His mouth tilted. "I like that wit, *bella*. I find myself regretting we only have tonight."

She tucked her chin and gave him an admonishing look. "You're patronizing me again. I don't need the rules spelled out. I'm not *that* green."

"See? Such sharp intelligence is the sort of thing that holds my interest longer than a few hours."

"Is that how long your liaisons usually last?"

He stopped dancing, arm remaining across her back, but loosely. "That's probably not a good topic of conversation."

"I know." Bubbles tickled her nose as she sipped, trying to wash away a strange bitterness on her tongue. It shouldn't matter what his past looked like. Whatever man eventually attached himself to her wouldn't come to her pristine. She couldn't expect it when she had such a complicated history herself. "I think I'm looking for reasons not to like you so I won't feel so…"

She frowned. The hand she'd rested on his shoulder slid down to splay on his chest as if she had the right to touch him with such familiarity, but touching him felt very natural. Her fingertips dipped beneath the ribbon of red, sliding the tips of her polished nails beneath it as she ever so slightly lifted it off the crispness of his shirt.

"I'm not a pushover. I'm normally the most contrary person you could imagine. A fighter." Her family told her that all the time, so why was she letting this happen? Her usual streak of rebellion was absent.

Actually, she realized with a spark of insight, it was directed against the life she'd been leading, pushing her to break free of old restraints. No one was stopping her from spending a night with a man except her. All she had to do was *choose* to.

"I'm not trying to pressure you. I'm sincere that I wish we had more time to get to know one another, but my life has never allowed for long term relationships." His hand shifted to splay in a warm brand against her lower back, offering a soothing caress. "For what it's worth—" He bit the inside of his cheek, seeming to weigh what he was about to say. The shadow moved behind his eyes again, telling her that he was uncomfortable with how revealing his words were. "If you walked out of here right now, I wouldn't go looking for someone else. You're the only woman I want to be with tonight."

"Why?" It came out of her with a pang of disbelief. "Please don't say it's because you like the way I look." She didn't want him to want Gili. It would break her heart—it really would.

His breath came out in a soft snort of disbelief. "Because of the way we make each other feel."

He lowered his head to graze his damp lips along her jaw and down to her neck, making her shiver. Her nipples pulled tight so quickly they stung. He chuckled softly at the way she audibly caught her breath.

"We're positively volatile." His hot breath bathed her ear before his teeth lightly closed on her lobe, nearly causing her knees to buckle.

She pressed her hand more firmly to his chest.

"No?" He drew back, but held her close. Held her up, if she was honest.

"I'm trying to think," she gasped, nearly overwhelmed by sensations that were the furthest thing from fear.

"And you can't? Then we feel the same." His tight smile only made the edgy fist of need inside her clench harder. "Feel, *bella*. Feel how much you're exciting me." He moved her hand all the way under the sash, so the pound of his heart slammed into her palm. "This isn't anything I've ever experienced, either."

Her scalp tingled. She dropped her champagne glass, ignoring the delicate break of crystal, wanting too badly to touch him with both hands. She slid her fingers to the back of his neck and raised her mouth, inviting him to kiss her. It was pure instinct and he didn't hesitate, covering her parted lips as though he'd been let off his leash after having been tempted for too long.

The world stopped then spun the other way, dizzying her. She made one whimpering noise, astonished by how thoroughly such a thing could devastate her, wilting all her muscles.

She distantly heard another delicate shatter, then he picked her up, lifting his head to reveal a fierce expression. Victory? Not quite, but there was something conquering there. Something exalted.

Yet his bright gaze asked a question.

She nodded, unable to speak, just gave herself up to it, to him. She knew when to fight her body and when to surrender. Perhaps it was the silver lining to all those years of having to accept that physiology trumped logic. This was bigger than anything she could make sense of.

He set her on the bed and she watched him throw off his jacket, shaken by the feelings that were carving a valley through her. He joined her and dragged her half under him, kissing her again. Thorough, drugging kisses that set her alight, yet she felt stiff and frozen.

"What's wrong?" He lifted his head, proving himself to be attuned to her in a way that was reassuring and disturbing all at once.

"I'm shy," she admitted, ducking her head as she said it because that wasn't her at *all*. Her eyes stung with emotive tears at how monumental this was. She was alone with a man, on a *bed*, and he had set the sun inside her. He made it radiate outward, filling her with such heat and joy she was going to burst. "I want to touch you, but I don't want to make a fool of myself. I don't know if I can contain myself."

"Don't even try." His voice brimmed with graveled warning, which might have made her chuckle, but she released her breath and let her hands move to greedily stake a claim.

He was firm everywhere, taut and strong. Hot. Her fingers discovered the textures of his clothes, then slid beneath his shirt as he yanked it free of his belted pants. He made an approving noise as she found satin skin and the tension of his abdomen, then the shape of his rib cage and the sleek muscles across his chest. The sharp beads of his nipples fascinated her.

She made her own appreciative noises, utterly

rapt with the contrast of his body to her own, all flat planes and crisp hair and indomitable strength.

He released her zip and dragged down the loosened front of her dress. As he bared her breasts, something elemental gripped her. The spirit of womanhood. She melted onto her back and arched, emphasizing their differences, liking that he made a noise that sounded almost suffering, yet growly and ferocious. He opened his mouth and engulfed her in such a place of earthy pleasure, she released her own cry of agonized joy.

*Volatile.* Was that what this was? She hadn't known she could feel like this, frantic yet intoxicated. Impatient yet timeless. She wanted to stay like this forever, running their hands over each other, kissing, mouths needing to fuse and breathing be damned. But as his hands moved on her, shifting silk with a touch so hot it burned her through the fabric, she wanted more. So much more.

His fingertips grazed the slit in her gown and she found herself offering more of her leg then trembling in anticipation, waiting for the feel of his touch on her skin. The pet of his hand on the outside of her thigh made her shiver. She gloried in the way he kissed her harder, deeper, hand shaping her hip, exploring her belly, then tracking to her other thigh. He squeezed the taut muscle then moved with delicious confidence to cup the center of her.

Breath stalling, eyes opening, she waited for panic, but before she could entertain a grim memory, he firmed his touch and rocked his hand, sending a jolt of incredible pleasure through her pelvis. Her eyelids grew heavy again and she found herself lifting, spellbound by the lightning bolts of sensation that grew in strength as they kissed and he caressed her.

How could anything feel this good?

She wanted to touch him as intimately, but she could hardly think of anything but how he was making her feel. Just as she tried to shape him through his pants, his touch changed, exploring beneath silk with knowledge and intention.

She bucked in reaction. "I can't—My heart is going to explode."

She moved a reflexive hand to cover his, not quite stopping him, because the slide of his fingers against her was so mesmerizing, but so sensitizing she almost couldn't bear it. Her entire focus narrowed to that delicate circle and stroke.

"I want to be inside you, but I don't want to stop touching you. Like that?" He pushed a long finger into her.

She couldn't speak, could only hear a keening noise that came from her as he penetrated and circled where she was so sensitive and molten that she ached. She tightened, trying to savor, trying to hold back the build, but wanton mindlessness took over. Her hips danced against his hand, the pleasure growing too acute to bear, tension growing and growing until she couldn't stand it—

"*Oh*!" Her world exploded in a sudden release that had her shaking and shuddering, flesh pulsing and eyes tearing at the absolute beauty of it.

She pressed his hand still, trying to ease the sensation, trying to catch her breath.

He kissed her, tongue questing for hers, and continued to gently caress her, soothing and teasing so her level of arousal didn't fade, only edged into deeper desire.

With a groan, she rolled into him, strangely ravenous. She wanted the barriers between them gone. Wanted *all of him*. What was he *doing* to her?

He made a feral noise and they tugged at each other's clothing, stripping in seconds, then rolled back together, naked, gloriously naked. Now he was hers, all hers. She swept her hands over him, enamored with his broad shoulders but equally fascinated by his rock-hard biceps and the way his Adam's apple bobbed in a swallow.

When she cradled the fiercest part of him in her palm, she wasn't frightened at all. She felt

powerful, especially when he looked agonized
and closed his eyes and breathed, *"Bella."*

With a smile, she pressed her mouth to his
throat and tried to roll him onto his back. He
rolled her beneath him instead, pressing over
her as he kissed her, letting her caress him as
he used his tongue to mimic what he wanted to
do until she couldn't take it and tore her mouth
from his. "I need—"

She didn't know what she needed. She was
restless and urgent, loins feeling achy and neglected. Empty.

He reached over to the night table then rose
over her, knees sliding between hers and parting her legs with effortless strength.

She felt so many things in that moment. Vulnerable, yes, but strangely trusting. It didn't matter if she didn't particularly enjoy this part. She
wanted to know she could take a man—

"Oh."

He paused, tip pressing for entry, the invasion
startling enough that she tensed.

His head came up. His whole body was taut,
his cheeks flushed, his eyes glittering, but there
was a shred of man still governing the animal.
"I might literally die if you've changed your
mind."

Maybe that's what made her smile. Maybe
it was the fact her body was so eager for his.

Maybe it was simply the joy of this crazy, magical night.

With a little arch, she invited him to complete his thrust and he did with a shudder, sinking deep, gaze never leaving hers, but glowing hot as the center of a flame as their flesh melded.

To say she became a woman under his possession was silly, but she *felt* like a woman in that moment. Mature and whole and *sacred*. She was responding exactly as nature intended under the advances of a mate. *Her* mate. With this act, he gave her back her sexuality, her desire. Her *self*.

She closed her eyes against something too big to contemplate, but it only made the sensations intensify as he took a testing withdraw and return. She shivered as though velvet passed over her skin.

"Yes?"

"Yes," she moaned, savoring the deliciousness that lingered with anticipation for another stroke. "More."

Lucidity faded as he did it again. And again.

He began to thrust with more purpose. She found her hips rising to meet his, longing for the return of his. Needing it. The dance delivered such acute pleasure, she released a strangled groan of enjoyment.

He picked up the tempo and magnificent sensations ran through her. She wanted to tell him but couldn't speak, as she was too enraptured. Tension gripped her. A kind of tortured ecstasy—her body searching for an answering call in his.

She needed him to be as driven beyond himself as she was. To come with her to this place where nothing existed but this new being they had become with their joining. Scraping her nails down his back, she grasped at his buttocks and pulled him into her. Into the eye of the storm.

They struck the pinnacle together, the climax so intense, she opened her mouth in a soundless scream. Pleasure like she had never known flooded in, drowning her as he held himself magnificently deep inside her, throbbing in her jubilant grip as he released a ragged cry of exhilaration and shuddered with completion.

Xavier swore.

"What's wrong?" Trella murmured, hands moving with endless appetite over his damp shoulders.

He withdrew and rolled away. "The condom broke."

She was glad it was dark now. After the first time, they had turned out the lights and slid under the covers to fondle and caress for ages, barely speaking, just kissing and enjoying.

Bonding, she might have been tempted to think, yet something in his silence, and the condoms in the night table, told her he had done this a lot.

She had suffered a hollow ache as she'd forced herself to accept that, despite his sweet words, she was merely the woman *du jour* for him. A lady of the night, really.

Whether he had sensed her withdrawal, or she was just that easy, he had grown more passionate. The second time had been even better than the first. Her inhibitions were gone and he held out, giving her two shattering orgasms before taking her on a third ride that nearly killed her, their shared climax being so powerful.

She was too sweaty and lethargic to be triumphant, but she was pretty darned smug at having taken a lover. She had distantly been hoping she had rocked his world as thoroughly as he had rocked hers, but reality struck like a brick through a window at his words.

"It's okay. I won't get pregnant." She swallowed, trying to clear the thickness that gathered in her throat.

"You're on the pill or something?"

Or something. "Yes."

"I have physicals all the time."

"I'm fine, too." Did people really have these conversations? It scraped the romance off a wonderful evening, leaving her thinking about the rest of reality. Guilt crawled in. She had kept secrets from him and—far worse—from her family. They'd be worried sick if they knew where she was.

As if on cue, her phone plinked with the harp notes of her sister's ringtone. Like some kind of empath, Angelique was picking up on her sudden discord.

"I have to get that," Trella murmured, then she groaned. Her muscles ached as though she'd run a marathon. She forced herself to rise and move naked across the shadowed room, finding her clutch where she'd dropped it in the lounge, then came back to the bedroom door.

She stayed there, slyly hoping he was looking at her, silhouetted by the lamplight. In a quick exchange of texts, she reassured her sister she was fine. Gili knew something was up, though. Tendrils of misgivings began working through Trella's system. It was time to call it a night. She needed to hole up at the flat where she knew she was completely safe and process all of this.

"I have to go." She clicked off her phone and sent him a smile of cheerful resignation.

"Is everything all right?" He rose to pull on his pants, not bothering with underwear, which pleased her for some reason, but he didn't invite her to stay, which depressed her as well.

"Just my sister. She needs me to get home."

She texted her guard that she would be ready in fifteen minutes and stepped into her thong.

Xavier shook out her gown and brought it to her, then moved behind her as she stepped into it. Hurrying her? She pulled up the gown then lifted her hair while he zipped.

His hands lingered on her skin, not moving, not holding her in place, but his grave words pinned her motionless. "I remember her kidnapping."

She dropped her arms, letting her hair fall over his hands, as helpless and as terrified as she had ever been. Her breastbone turned to ice and her ears strained to hear what he would say next.

"I was fourteen. My father was renouncing the crown. My mother was already gone, exiled by my grandmother for their divorce. I was feeling very sorry for myself. Then I saw photos of this little girl, so pretty and happy, stolen. I stopped worrying what would happen to me. I was so relieved when she was recovered."

His fingertips stayed across her shoulders, not caressing, just resting in small hot prints. She thought she would bruise from the contact. Not in a painful way. It was the opposite of injury. Healing?

He drew in a sharp breath and pulled his touch from her skin. "I don't know why I said that. It was far too personal for both of us. You're clearly still worried about her if you're rushing off." He bent to retrieve her shoes. "I hope she's all right."

*It was me.* She should have said it, but her throat was too tight.

She knew there were people who had rooted for her family all the way along, but it was so wrapped up in their notoriety, she didn't differentiate the kindly meant from the intrusive or downright cruel. Her family hadn't asked to be famous for the odd trick of nature that had created two sets of identical twins. They were just people, perhaps better looking by certain standards, definitely richer than average, but regular humans.

Yet the world was insatiably curious about what brand of soap they used and held strong opinions on how they should conduct themselves.

To have this man, who was completely removed from it, reveal such a personal memory connected to her affected her, changing the careful constructs inside her. Defenses that held darkness at bay while keeping her open to the people who loved her shifted and angled to provide space for him to enter.

*No.* She couldn't let him in! Tie herself to a man? Lose herself behind someone else's goals and wishes and expectations when she had so many unreached aspirations of her own? She couldn't attach herself to someone whose life was bigger than hers. She was trying to escape all the restraints that had bound her for so long.

Shaken at how vulnerable she was to him, she jiggled her bodice against her breasts, then perched on a chair to strap on her shoes, hands trembling.

"Is she really as beautiful as you?" He watched her with his fists pushed into his pockets. His naked shoulders were relaxed and outlined in pale gold while the shadows in his face suggested a brooding expression. The dark patch of his chest hair narrowed to a suggestive line, arrowing to his navel, then lower.

He was the beautiful one. She memorized this last intimate glimpse of him.

"Exactly as beautiful." She smiled, amused with her own joke, then poignant gratitude accosted her. "Thank you for tonight. I—" She stopped herself from saying something truly gauche.

She wanted to ask if he'd meant it when he'd said it wasn't always like this for him. She wanted to tell him what he had given her. She wanted to get out of here before she revealed too much.

She glanced at the clock. If she didn't show her face promptly, her guard would knock and enter. They were paid very well to be diligent and investigate when she wasn't where she said she would be.

Xavier moved to offer a hand, helping her to her feet. "Thank *you*. This was lovely." The words came off lighthearted, punching into her as she imagined the legions of other women who had heard such offhand praise. Not even, *I won't forget you*. Just, *this was lovely*. A pleasant meal. Nothing life-changing.

He brought her hand to his mouth, exactly as he had when they'd met, except this time he turned her hand over and kissed her palm.

Trying to hide how deeply that affected her, she said, "Goodnight, sweet Prince."

He snorted. "I could have you beheaded for that."

With a lightning move, he pulled her close and wove his fingers into her hair, planting a real kiss, a final one, on her mouth. It was painfully sweet. Thorough, yet tender. Oddly heartbreaking.

For her.

And even though she was the one to draw back, her lips clung to his. Temptation to stay, to say more, gripped her, but he distracted her.

"You've lost an earring." His fingertip flicked at her lobe.

"No!" Both hands went to her ears, finding one empty. "Here? In the room? Did you notice if I had both while we were downstairs?"

"I'll buy you new ones," he offered with an offhand shrug.

"They're sentimental. A gift from my father." *To Gili.* She clicked on the lamp and flung back the bed covers, searching.

A polite knock tapped on the main door, her guard telling her the car was in position. They avoided waiting whenever possible. It drew a crowd.

"I'll find it and send it to you at the design house."

"Promise?" She looked from his muscled chest to the sheets to his eyes. Oh, he was spectacular in the golden light, emptying her brain all over again.

"I only make promises I can keep."

"Thank you." She didn't bother worrying about him addressing it to Angelique. She would intercept it or come clean if she had to. "I really did, um, enjoy this."

His eyes warmed with laughter. "My pleasure, *bella.*"

She was starting to sound like the neophyte she was. Definitely time to make her escape. She ducked her head and made for the coach before she turned into a pumpkin.

# CHAPTER THREE

*Present day...*

COMMUNICATIONS FROM PRINCE XAVIER'S grandmother fell into three categories. All were delivered by the palace's Private Secretary, Mario de Gaul.

"Your grandmother requests a meeting to discuss…" Fill in the blank. Those were routine and benign. She listened to her grandson's opinions and they worked together on a strategy for whatever event, negotiation or dignified visitor stood on the horizon. They were equals, more or less.

The second, more ominous type of appointment began with "Her Majesty invites you to join her at…" Fill in the meal. Those were more dictatorial instructions on how she wanted something handled. A parliamentarian or ambassador needed massaging. A high-level staff member needed firing. He was doing her dirty work.

Then there was—

"The Queen is in her receiving room. She expects you."

Mario entered with that missive on the heels of Xavier's Personal Assistant, who still stood before him, his speech bubble of grim news dissolving in the air above his pleading don't-shoot-the-messenger expression.

"Of course." Xavier rose from his desk. It was the appropriate response. One didn't refuse the Queen. One certainly didn't leave her waiting.

Still, his agile brain leapt to all the triage he needed to accomplish in the next few minutes, not least of which was to reassure his new fiancée, Patrizia, before she saw the headlines herself.

*Switched Before Birth!*
*Future King an Expectant Father?*
*Trella Tricked Everyone—Including*
*the Prince!*

He should have said something a few weeks ago, of course, when the first bomb went off. Trella Sauveterre, lately returned to the public eye, had turned up pregnant. The reaction had been loud enough to shake the world off its axis, forcing him to reach out to her, again, much to his dismay. He didn't want anything to do with her after realizing how thoroughly she'd duped him.

*Why had she done it?*

The sting of chasing her to Berlin a week after Paris, like a fool with his first crush, came back hot and fresh under his skin. He'd had a very real duty to meet with Patrizia, but he had put it off, stealing an extra few days of bachelorhood, inventing excuses so he could…what? Have sex with a stranger once more?

Sex was sex. He'd had many lovers over the years and experienced varied degrees of pleasure. He put down the better experiences to chemistry, the less satisfying ones to inhibitions and incompatibility.

That night in Paris had seemed extraordinary while it was happening. She hadn't been a virgin, but she'd made sex feel new again. She'd been so responsive. So sensual. So *abandoned.* His stomach tightened just remembering it.

*So what?* He knew from his father's history that letting the brain below his belt do his thinking was disastrous.

Nevertheless, a day later, when he had read that *Angelique* would be in Berlin, he had reconfigured his entire schedule. Rather than courier her earring as promised, he had sought her out— only to find her with another man.

It had been the most lowering of moments, not because his ego was dented, but because he had revealed something of himself to her. Somehow, she had tricked him into believing they had a connection that went beyond the physical. What had possessed him to talk of those dark hours when his parents had been banished?

He didn't form intimate friendships. He was an only child raised by a grandmother whose life was too demanding to offer affection. Yet, for some reason, he had entrusted a one-night lover with his private thoughts.

He had trusted *her*. When she had said she didn't sleep around, he had believed her.

Judging by what he found in Berlin, however, she'd moved on very quickly. The innocent act was part of her routine, he had concluded, castigating himself for acting so callow as to follow her.

Nevertheless, when he had the chance to catch her alone, he approached, waiting for the catch of excitement she had kindled in him the week before.

Nothing. She was desirable the way all beautiful women were, but whatever he'd felt in Paris was gone. It had perplexed and annoyed him, made him doubly irritated with himself for thinking they'd had something special.

He's stood there searching for whatever it was that he'd found so enthralling and she had pretended she didn't even know him, staring blankly as though he had broken into her bedroom and stolen the diamond hoop earring he was returning.

In those seconds, he had felt as though she was even more of a stranger than she had been before they'd made love—which she was, he promptly learned. He hadn't slept with Angelique. He had slept with her twin, Trella.

The revelation had been welcome and infuriating. He didn't care for dishonest people, but his desire to see Trella had renewed itself. He had asked Angelique to pass along his contact details, wanting an explanation. Wanting something he refused to acknowledge, but...

Nothing.

Not one returned call, message or text.

What did it matter? He made himself get over her, focusing on more important things, primarily his duty to marry.

He had made a concerted effort to avoid all headlines containing the name Sauveterre, which wasn't easy. First, the mysterious, reclusive Trella had come out at a friend's wedding. That had kept the gossip industry booming through spring and summer, along with other news within the family, making it a challenge for him to change channels or flick screens fast enough to avoid catching sight of her.

Then, just as things seemed to have died down, she'd been caught climbing from her brother's car looking less svelte than in previous photos. *Pregnant*, the avid Sauveterre watchers speculated.

So what if she was? It didn't make a hill of beans difference to anyone's life, least of all his.

Still, Xavier had looked closely at the photos that emerged, one showing her in a stunning maternity gown at her brother's engagement party. She didn't look *very* pregnant. She had said she was on the pill. If she was carrying his child, she would have returned his calls. He didn't have anything to worry about, he assured himself.

This latest inflammatory sound bite was more of the same. Had to be. He had a walk-on part in the episodic drama that was the Sauveterre serial. He had slept with her *one night*. He resented being drawn into scandal for it. He was now engaged. That made besmirching his name unforgiveable. Immediately after allaying his grandmother's concern, he would insist Trella clear him of involvement so he could reassure Patrizia their marriage plans could continue.

Damn it, he had completely forgotten about Patrizia. He paused to text.

I'll have this cleared up shortly.

Their match was perfect in every way. Not only would it strengthen both of their countries, but they liked each other. Neither had unrealistic notions like love and passion to muddy the waters. She was nursing a bruised heart and was keen for a stable, reliable situation. A civilized relationship, she kept calling it.

He was pleased to perform his duty in a way he could stand. Patrizia was intelligent, attractive, well-bred. She would have children for the same reason he would: They were expected to. They respected one another. They were on the same page.

*He wanted this marriage.*

Mario paused with him and knocked, then announced him.

His grandmother didn't rise as Xavier entered. She didn't even look up from whatever she was writing with her antique silver pen. The crackle in the fireplace became the only sound along with the scratch of her pen.

He took the bull by the horns. "I'll refute it and press charges against the source."

The pen went down and she peered at him over her glasses. She was a well-preserved seventy, her eyes were the same Deunoro blue as his own, her hair more iron than silver. She was overdue to start her morning audiences, which always made her salty.

"The Queen Mother of Zhamair is the source."

Xavier's PA had also pointed out that the

story had stemmed from Angelique's soon-to-be mother-in-law. "I haven't had a chance to confirm that. If she made a statement, I'm sure it's in reaction to some online nonsense."

"She is reacting, I am informed, to remarks made about her son and his fiancée. She wanted to set the record straight that Angelique was not the woman kissing you in the photos that emerged some months ago from Paris. Angelique has always been faithful to King Kasim. Is that true?"

"I couldn't say whether she's been faithful, but I'm told I was with Trella."

"You were *told*?"

"They're twins." He shrugged, not bothering to feel awkard discussing his sex life with his grandmother. She had had "The Talk" with him herself when he was an adolescent, explaining in no uncertain terms that royalty did *not* produce bastards and had offered explicit tips on how to prevent such a thing.

"That particular twin is pregnant." She used her most imperious tone. "A source intimately connected to her family has stated you were with her at an appropriate time for conception. Did you take precautions?"

"Of course."

*The condom broke. Are you on the pill?*
*Yes.*

"She would have told me if there were consequences." Tension gathered in the pit of his gut. He didn't know which one of them he was trying to convince. "Any woman who sets out to trap a man does not hide it for six months. Even if it was an accident, there's no reason to keep it from me. She might be pregnant, but *it's not mine*."

Her brows went up in regal disdain. "Perhaps you should confirm that."

As if that hadn't occurred to him? "Of course," he said. Dutifully.

"Because it would be a shame if this were to cause any delay in our schedule." She intended to step down the minute he was married. To Patrizia.

"Understood."

It was hot in Innsbruck, despite the elevation and the calendar showing the last days of summer. But maybe the heat was caused by this extra human she was carrying.

Trella lifted her face into the gentle breeze, enjoying the sweet scent of it. She was six months along and felt it, even though she wasn't showing much. Her mother had possessed the same tall, model-slender figure and had barely shown with twins until the very end. This was only one and with the right clothes, she barely looked pregnant.

She needed that ambiguity. Prince Xavier's texts had devolved to the two-word kind.

Call me.

She had ignored the latest, received this morning, exactly as she'd ignored every other text and call she'd received from him, the first immediately after he'd met Angelique in Berlin, and most recently after she'd been exposed by her sister's soon-to-be mother-in-law as the twin in his arms at the ball in Paris.

She had her reasons. That's what she kept telling herself, even though it was pure emotion that drove her and that emotion was cowardice.

"They're blocked by a service vehicle," her guard, Benita, said of their car, lifting her gaze from her phone to continue her scan of the street. "Let's wait inside."

Benita was as tall as Trella and had a mannish demeanor when she was on the job. No nonsense, no makeup, hair scraped into a bun, communications terse.

Trella didn't mind. She wasn't the most cooperative principal. To her occasional chagrin, she was a high maintenance person in every way. Acknowledging that about herself didn't stop her from saying, "I'd rather stay out here."

The day was gorgeous and she would be on

bed rest soon. She wanted to enjoy the outside world while she could.

"Killian said—"

"I know. Take extra precautions." She scoffed at a lot of things, but not security reports. "I spoke to Sadiq. He's the one who discovered the hack and restored all the firewalls. No one even knows I'm here."

Except the handful of people inside the building who had just taken selfies with her. They were no doubt posting those as she spoke. She was a celebrity, whether she liked it or not. It was only a matter of minutes before lookie-loos began pulling over, wanting their own photo with a Sauveterre, especially the elusive pregnant one.

"My gut doesn't like it."

"Because Killian trains you to be overprotective."

Benita had tried to cancel this trip as soon as the security bulletin had come through. Trella wasn't sure why she had insisted on making what amounted to a house call for a joint venture she wasn't sure she would pursue, but she had.

Ah, she knew why she had come. For starters, her sister had been doing this kind of thing on her behalf for years. It was yet another burden she had placed on her twin and it was her turn to pay it back, now that Angelique was starting her life with Kasim.

Oh, her sister was in love. It was as majestic a sight to behold as the timeless sparkling peaks around them. Trella was deeply happy for her, but so very envious.

Her gaze tracked to the sharpest, highest peaks to the south. To Elazar.

Was he texting from inside that border, sitting in his palace office, cursing her for ignoring him?

A flutter in her midsection had her resisting the urge to press her hand across her belly. She didn't like to draw attention to her pregnancy when she was in public. Besides, it wasn't the baby that caused that stir in her middle. It was a complex mix of emotions.

She wanted to tell him she was grateful. She wanted to see him again, to discover if the magical connection she'd felt in Paris had been real or just a product of an exciting foray into independence. She wanted him to know they were expecting a baby.

She also wanted to hold their night in her memory as the ideal that it was. She didn't want the harsh fallout she would have to face once she acknowledged this baby as his. Most of all, she didn't want to be a burden on a man who had seemed too perfect to want anything to do with someone as flawed as she was.

Her expected black sedan with its darkened windows slid up to the curb.

"There. See?" Trella said, even as she noted a man approaching in her periphery.

"That's not—" Benita's voice cut off.

Perhaps Trella went deaf at that moment because nothing penetrated beyond the fact that the back door opened and the Prince of Elazar rose from the interior.

He was as remarkable as she remembered. Like a knight of legend, his hair shot with glints of gold, his visage sharp and stern, his air one of heroic power. He was so godlike, she couldn't move. She was too mesmerized.

Then reality rushed in as a scuffling noise and a grunt penetrated. She swung her gaze to see Benita in a fight. A *fight*. With a *man*. He tried to twist Benita's arm behind her back as she bent forward, trying to use leverage to flip him.

Training, the kind Trella had attended to daily until pregnancy had sent her into yoga and water aerobics, jolted her into action. As Benita's attacker pulled back his weight, dragging Benita off her feet, Trella stepped in and nailed him with a solid, knuckle-bruising punch, right in the nose.

The man grunted and Benita twisted, nearly escaping.

"What the *hell* are you doing?" That *accent*. Strong hands grasped her upper arms and pulled her away from the struggling pair.

Trella turned into him, stomach flip-flopping

in response as she felt his solid abdomen against her bump. Adrenaline coursed through her, but she only felt reassurance as he drew her protectively close. Her gaze stayed over her shoulder, fixed on the fight, which seemed to be more of a wrestle for dominance. A bloody nose wasn't slowing down the man and Benita wasn't giving up, biting out in Spanish, "Run."

"Help her—Wait. What are *you* doing?" Trella cried as she realized she was being shoved into the back of the car.

Xavier easily overpowered her, pushing her in and following without ceremony.

She was so shocked that it took her a moment to resist. By then his big body had created a wall of shoulders and chest that were impossible to get past.

Before she could touch the door on her side, he pulled his own closed and the locks clicked. The car pulled away, leaving her guard scrapping on the sidewalk with a brute whose shirt was the same color as both men in the front of this car.

Far too late, she realized what was happening. She was being kidnapped. *Again*.

# CHAPTER FOUR

"STOP THIS CAR. *Now.*"

Xavier respected her ability to sound so authoritative, but he ignored her and opened the privacy window long enough to accept an ice pack from his physician, Gunter, then tapped the button to close it.

"Hello, Trella. Have I got that right?" He knew he had the right one. It was impossible to explain, but the minute he had seen her, he had known.

He pushed aside the ridiculous high that rocketed through him as he finally had her alone and held out his palm. He wiggled his fingers, urging her to release the pendant she was pinching and let him examine her hand.

"What were you thinking, getting involved in that?" The mix of rage and fear he'd experienced at seeing her step into the fight was reflected in his tone. Even if she wasn't pregnant, it would have been a foolhardy, dangerous thing to do.

But she was pregnant. There was no denying it. The narrow waist he'd held in the crook of his arm had thickened with an undeniable bump. Her breasts…

He dragged his gaze up, refusing to let fantasies sidetrack him, but her features were a distraction all on their own. Her face was rounder, her mouth lush and pouted. The urge to kiss her struck him with a fierce pull.

Damn it, what *was* it about her?

He met her glare with his own, thinking that he would have sworn her eyes were green, but they were steely. Bright as a cornered cat refusing to stay that way.

"I thought I was preventing myself from being kidnapped. Once again, I have trusted the wrong person." Her unpainted lips seemed bloodless, which gave him a moment of pause, but too much of his life had been set off balance by her. He wanted answers. Today.

"It's not a kidnapping." He set the ice pack near her thigh. "It's an improvised meeting to discuss mutual business, so drop your pendant. I know it's a tracking device. Your guard won't be harmed, only delayed. Your car can't chase us. It's still blocked."

"Which sounds a lot like a kidnapping." A harsh ringtone emanated from her purse. "That's for you." She pulled out her phone and used her thumbprint to accept the call then handed it to Xavier. Her hand might have trembled.

Desperate times called for desperate measures, he'd told himself when he'd concocted this intervention. As he picked up on Trella's shaken nerves, he wondered if he was using a sledgehammer to kill a fly. It hadn't occurred to him she might be anything but angry at having her timetable interrupted. He couldn't be happier if he inconvenienced the hell out of her. He was beyond incensed at the way she was impacting his life without any attempt to mitigate it.

Explaining that would have to wait. He'd been warned to expect this video call. He took the phone and met the formidable expression of a man who resembled Trella. Henri, Xavier suspected, since the other brother was in Brazil.

"Your demands?" Henri asked without greeting.

"A blood sample for a DNA test."

Trella made a strangled noise. "Like hell."

He glanced at her. "I would accept her word as to whether she's carrying my heir, but she's lied to me more than once already."

Xavier willed her to lash out with denials of his paternity. With an explanation. An *apology*.

She hitched her chin and turned her face to the window.

"Return her to where you took her. I'll see what I can do about the blood test."

"You can't even get her to return a call. I can't wait any longer."

Trella's silence was gut-knottingly damning. Whatever lingering favor he had felt toward her went ashen and bitter. A jagged lump hardened in his throat. He swallowed it, but the acrimony only moved to burn as a hot knot behind his collarbone. Each minute that she failed to deny his paternity was a tiny, incremental progression toward accepting what he had been refusing to believe. What he still didn't want to believe.

"I have your coordinates," Henri said, dragging Xavier back from staring at the woman who was ruining his life. "A team has been dispatched. We don't need an incident. Return her to Innsbruck."

"If you're tracking us, you know we'll be in Elazar soon." Xavier leaned toward the window to see a helicopter chasing from the distance. "I'll close the borders if I have to, but she's perfectly safe, especially if that's our future monarch inside her. Stand down from trying to stop us."

"Unless my sister gives me her safe word, this escalates."

Xavier handed her the phone. "Your move, *bella*."

She flashed him a sharp glance then looked at her brother.

"We're coming," Henri said.

"I know." She nodded, pale and grave, then said, "Begonia."

*"Vous êtes certain?"*

*"Sí."*

"That's tomorrow's word," Xavier said.

She shot him a startled frown.

He shrugged. "I do my homework."

"Then you'll know I'm buying you twenty-four hours." She turned back to her phone, expression haughty. "I'm sure Killian knows by now who hacked him. Ask him to drop a virus into the Elazar palace networks, won't you?"

"Killian has Elazar's Minister of Foreign Affairs on the phone, along with a more aggressive team assembled."

Xavier suspected that remark was more for his benefit.

*"Gracias.* Tell him I'll handle it."

"Will you?"

A leaden silence followed where she only gave her brother a tight-lipped look.

Xavier wondered if others were also frustrated by the avoidance game she had been playing.

*"Bien,"* Henri said. "If I don't hear from you every hour, your prince may expect a gun against his temple. *Je t'aime."*

*"Te amo."* She ended the call and slipped her phone back into her purse, then folded her hands

into her lap. "Why did you say I lied to you more than once?"

Xavier admired the way she attempted to take control of the conversation, but he was not prepared to give her any concessions until he had what he wanted.

"Why did you speak Spanish and he, French? Was it code?"

"Habit."

She tried to leave it there, but he lifted a skeptical brow.

"It's true. Our father was French, Mama is Spanish. We grew up speaking both. I only told one lie."

"That you were on birth control."

"That I was Angelique. You asked if I was on the pill *or something*. I said yes because that was true. At least, I thought it was." She bit the corner of her lip.

"Your *or something* failed?"

She flinched, making him realize his voice carried a thickness close to contempt or even hatred.

He grappled to hang onto his temper. "You assured me pregnancy wasn't possible. How have we arrived at having this conversation?"

Dumb question. They both knew how babies were made. They'd made love. She had come apart in his arms again and again. He'd been greedy as a starved beast certain he would die from the pleasure of being inside her when she shattered around him like that. Then, when he couldn't hold back any longer, he had joyously thrown himself into the small death of simultaneous orgasm.

In that post-climactic moment, when her breaths had still been jagged and his heart had pounded against her sweating breasts, he had felt...restored. Not just a release of tension but as though deeper needs had been met. Withdrawing had provoked a painful, abandoned sensation he had impatiently tried to forget.

*"Is that my child?"*

She jolted at the grate in his tone. "You said you wouldn't believe me no matter what I said."

"You'll submit to a blood test, then?"

Her eyes narrowed in mutiny.

"You can submit nicely or I can pin you down while my doctor takes it." He was clearly a sadist because something in him longed for her to push him into restraining her.

"Touch me and I'll break *your* nose." She started to lift a threatening fist and flinched, quickly cradling her right hand—which is what she'd been doing since her hands had gone into her lap, he realized.

He caught her wrist and held on when she tried to pull away. The backs of her fingers were an angry red, her knuckles puffy.

His heart lurched.

"Did you break any bones? Can you move your fingers? That's what this is for." He picked up the ice pack, incensed all over again that she had waded into the fight.

"I know how to throw a punch." She took the ice and flexed her fingers against it, showing only a wince of discomfort so he presumed she hadn't fractured anything.

"What were you thinking? It's a damned good thing his reflexes didn't take over. You would have been on the ground."

"My bodyguard was being assaulted."

"No, *my* bodyguard was moving into position to cover *me*. *She* attacked *him*. Then you did. Do you understand what bodyguards are paid to do? There is no reason you should have involved yourself."

Her brows flicked in dismissal of his concern.

Was this really the mother of his heir? If he'd gone to a brothel and bought a *man*, he couldn't have picked someone less suitable.

"A simple blood test could prove I'm not the father. We could have it done before we cross the border." He pointed at the sign they passed that stated they were less than a mile away.

"I'm afraid of needles."

"Be afraid of *me, bella*."

Her flat smile died. Something vulnerable flashed in her expression.

His conscience pinched.

"Is that the problem?" His voice still sounded gruff and aggressive. His animosity hadn't evaporated just because he was finally getting answers. He didn't want to soften toward her at all. She was far too dangerous. But fear was an explanation he could understand.

"Have you been afraid of my reaction? I'm not happy." That was a gross understatement. A well-practiced aloof demeanor had always served him well, but it was impossible to find in the face of this life-altering situation. Still, he tried to reassure her. "Nothing bad will happen if the baby is mine. I'll recognize him or her as our future monarch. We will marry so it's legitimate. That's all. No stake burnings or feeding to dragons. Were you afraid I'd pressure you to terminate? Is that why you've kept it from me?"

Silence. She turned her attention out the side window again, so he couldn't read her expression.

"Do you not *know* who the father is? How many contenders are there?"

Her glare swung like a blade to slice through him.

"I don't *care* how many men you've slept with." Much. He was disturbed to realize he did, actually. It wasn't because of the paternity question, either. The passion between them had been unprecedented. He didn't like to think she reacted that way to every man she slept with. It would have made all of this even more intolerable.

"How pregnant are you? Let's see if that eliminates me, shall we?"

"Pregnant enough to need a pit stop. Can we stop here?"

"No." The border guard waved them through with only a very minor slowing of their speed, recognizing the plates. "We'll be at my chalet shortly."

The car sped along the pass that formed part of the border between Austria and Elazar. As they rounded a bend, the valley opened, allowing a glimpse of Lirona, the capital, once a modest fiefdom, now a thriving city of culture, intellect and wealth. It sat like a heart against the shore of Lac Lirona, the arms of the mountains stretching out to embrace the blue water he loved with everything in him.

Over the centuries, his ancestors had fought to maintain their governance over this small kingdom many times. His great-grandmother had taken up with one of Hitler's top advisors to keep the Nazi invasion at occupation rather than annihilation.

*That is where the bar is set when it comes to duty,* his grandmother had extolled as a history lesson, explaining why Xavier's father was unfit to rule. *We are custodians. We do what we must. To put yourself before Elazar is treason.*

This, because his father had followed his libido into a high-profile affair with a topless waitress from Amsterdam then married the woman's aunt, owner of a drug café. His divorce from Xavier's mother had already been ugly and, even worse in his grandmother's eyes, *common.*

His grandmother was a hard woman—her father, King Ugo, hadn't forgiven his wife and Queen Julia had grown up in a harsh climate of blame and sacrifice. If her spare had survived, things might have been different. Instead, she had forced her only son to renounce the throne, disowning him and keeping her grandson as Elazar's future.

It was all on Xavier to perpetuate the monarchy into the next generation. He had planned to do so through an elegant association with Patrizia, a respected princess with a degree in social justice and a pedigree that couldn't be faulted.

Instead, he had behaved as impulsively as his father, tangling with a fashion designer whose life was stained with one scandal after another.

He was running out of hope that her child was not his. Whether his grandmother could find it in her to forgive him for this transgression didn't matter.

He would never forgive himself.

# CHAPTER FIVE

As someone who had grown up in obscene wealth, Trella didn't bat an eye at the chalet that turned out to be a three-story modern fortress with a nod to its rustic ancestors in its gables and tiered verandas.

She was more interested in counting pairs of eyes—one at the gate, two at the door, the physician who followed them into the house, the chauffeur who took the car around to what she presumed was the garage, a butler who greeted them and a woman named Inga who was asked to prepare tea.

"Powder room?" Trella clung by her fingernails to control.

Ghosts—terrible, terrible ghosts—were creeping in at the edges of her consciousness, but something pressured to diamond brightness inside her kept her from becoming hysterical. *This time she would get away.*

As each of the Prince's attempts to draw her out had pulled at her laser-like focus, she had resentfully allowed that she was taking the rough road, not the high one. She could still call in a team to break her out if she wanted, but a furious, too often helpless, part of her demanded she prove she could rescue herself.

Over the last months, she had come close many times to calling him. The problem was, she wasn't as stupid as many would conclude from her behavior. She knew what would happen and he had confirmed it. He would marry her.

Which meant a profile in the public eye that was even higher than the one she already occupied. One from which she couldn't retreat at will.

Worse, it meant being honest with him. She would have to reveal exactly how crazy she was. She would have to explain these ghouls tickling across her skin, making her want to scratch herself all over. The nightmare could spring to life with a beat of her heart, the cold sweats and shaking, the profound helplessness…

She hadn't suffered an attack since well before their night in Paris, but one ticked like a bomb inside her. She could feel it. But *no*. She wouldn't succumb, even though fighting it made it worse. She knew that.

With a dry mouth, she locked herself into a bathroom that smelled of potpourri. The small space was pristine, with a porcelain sink in a cherry wood vanity. She glanced from the full bath and shower to the frosted window that, once carefully opened, looked out onto the woods at the back of the house.

No balcony below this window, but it was big enough to allow a woman with a modest six month swelling in her middle to crawl through, and close enough to the nearby balcony she could swing a leg that direction and clamber across.

Not a kidnapping? Damned right it wasn't.

"I'm sure she'll come around," Xavier told Gunter. He hadn't lied when he had threatened to hold her down, but he didn't want to. It wasn't his habit to manhandle any woman, pregnant or otherwise. "Did she look six months to you?"

Gunter shook his head. "It's difficult to say. Every woman carries differently. The fact she was able to hide it so long leads me to wonder, but…"

They needed a blood test.

"And this?" Xavier waved to where she had disappeared to use the toilet.

"Extremely common. Although…" He glanced at his watch.

That's what Xavier had thought. He hadn't taken his eyes from the closed door and she was still in there. He didn't want to be indelicate, but he moved to knock.

Silence.

Fainted? His heart swerved.

"Trella." He tried the handle, found it locked and rattled it. "She wouldn't have—" The window dropped about thirty-two feet to the ground. That's why he hadn't bothered assigning someone to watch that side of the chalet.

"I'll send someone to check." Gunter hurried away, moving through the kitchen as Inga appeared with keys and a concerned expression.

Xavier gave the key a hard twist and walked into an empty powder room. A fresh breeze came through the open window. He glanced out to see Gunter below, holding Trella's clutch, a grim expression on his face as he tracked the distance to the nearest balcony.

At least *she* wasn't lying in the dirt below. Tramping through the alps in trendy heels wasn't much better. Damn it, this woman was turning into a nightmare.

"Alert security," he told Inga, and he strode outside to join the search.

Crammed beneath the sink was a little too much like the horrid cellar she'd been locked in during her first kidnapping. The shelf had easily moved to the bottom of the vanity, making room for her to curl herself on top of it, but she'd had to cover herself with the towels and was overheating.

Panicking.

No. One minute at a time. *Uno naranjo, dos*

*naranjos*... She counted the seconds, counted the oranges, a scent she always associated with family since they had a grove of them at Sus Brazos. She would get through this. It was another test of her ability to move on from her past.

She did her breathing exercises while she listened for footsteps. When she was confident everyone had moved outside, she carefully opened the cupboard door and groped her way out of the small space, thankful for her yoga practice.

Carrying her shoes, she paused at the door. There were security cameras. She had noted one in the foyer as they'd entered. Someone would be watching the screens. She had to move fast, but—*thank you, Killian*—she had what amounted to an SOS flare in her phone. It was supposed to be for signaling help, but she hoped it could have another use.

She took the device from her bra, turned on the blinding white light, and walked into the hall, aiming the beam directly at the first camera she came to. It sat like a brilliant spotlight on the dark orb. She prayed it blinded the lens as she hurried through the house to the garage.

There was no one in the kitchen and keys hung neatly on the hook beside the door. She tucked her phone back into her bra and took all the keys, deducing from a keychain which one belonged to the top-down cobalt blue Audi.

Outside the garage doors, she heard footsteps jogging across gravel.

Her entire body trembled, but she fought to keep a focused mind. She *wasn't* helpless. She *would* get away.

She set all the keys on the passenger seat and climbed behind the wheel of the Audi, then hit the button on the visor to open the garage door, ready to start the car as soon as the door climbed high enough.

There was a click, the hum of a motor and a rattle of effort, but the door didn't budge. She jabbed her finger onto the button again, glancing at the jumble of keys. Should she take a different car?

The door to the interior of the chalet opened and Xavier came into the shadowed garage.

*Nooooo!* She jabbed again and again at the stupid button, then started the car with a roar of its high-performance engine.

"The house is locked down. Don't try to drive through the door. It's reinforced. You'll hurt yourself. And my car." He moved past the other three vehicles with smooth steps, pausing beside her to lean in and turn off the engine, pocketing the key. "But that was a very good try. I'm impressed."

She gripped the steering wheel, staring straight ahead, concentrating on not revealing the tears gathering hotly behind her eyes.

"Come back into the house."

"No."

"We'll talk here then." He moved to flick a switch on the wall. A fan came to life with a low drone, quickly sucking away the lingering exhaust.

He came back to set an elbow on the top of the windscreen. She felt his eyes studying her, but kept her nose pointed forward.

"I'm trying to be patient, *bella*, I really am, but I don't understand why you're being so combative. This doesn't have to be a fight."

"I could drive this, you know. Probably better than you."

"Not without keys."

"You'd be surprised." She worked her hands on the steering wheel's soft leather, more than a little enamored with cars, thanks to Ramon. "I can hotwire and drive anything. I've been up to two hundred and twenty on a closed circuit in my brother's Pur Sang. The Gs nearly crack my ribs when I brake from that speed, but it's quite a rush. Have you ever driven this the way it was designed to drive?"

"No." His tone was one of forced patience.

"Ramon got into racing after taking evasive driving lessons. We all had to take them." Like Ramon, she had tried to outrun herself on the track more than once, but it was never a permanent solution. At some point, she had to park the car, take off the helmet and face reality. "Because of my kidnapping."

She sensed him grow very still, indicating she had his full attention.

Had he thought that wouldn't come up? She hated that it defined her, but it did. She worked around it as often as she could, but when she did have to face it, she did it head-on with her foot to the floor, even though it also had the power to crack her ribs and shatter everything inside her.

As the silence lengthened, she suspected he was reviewing what he had said in Paris—when he had thought he was talking about her but had been speaking *to* her.

"You think *you* were worried when I was stolen." Her voice trembled against her will. She soothed herself by running light fingers across the bumps in the bottom of the steering wheel, playing over them like keys on a piano, but her hands shook.

His voice was grave. "If I was triggering you today, you should have said."

"Really?" A smile touched lips that felt so dry they might split. Her body vibrated with fight-or-flight. She was going to crash hard after this, but she couldn't think about that yet. "Because I did tell you to take me back and you ignored me. Which is exactly what happened the first time."

Her knuckles whitened where she grasped the wheel again, trying to keep a grip on herself. It was time for the head-on collision.

"I said *stop*, and *no*, and *please* so many times I lost count. I said it when they threw me in their van and I could see Ramon running after us. I said it when one of them pulled me onto his lap and shoved his hand under my skirt and *hurt* me. I said it when he slapped me because I was fighting him. I said it when he locked me in a cold, dark cellar and I said it a lot when he let me out three days later, only to put me on a filthy stinking mattress and call me lucky. *Lucky*. Because he was going to show me what men liked."

She knew it was an assault to throw that at him. It was one of the reasons she rarely spoke about it, but she wanted to hurt him. She wanted to *scar* him.

"I should check with my therapist, see if my experience of being assaulted might create a profound desire to control my own destiny. Gosh, what an enlightening moment of self-discovery you've provided, Xavier. Yes, I'm quite sure that's why I'm *combative*."

He couldn't move, wasn't even sure he was breathing, as he tried to un-hear what she'd said. Who would do such a thing? To a *child*?

He didn't have a particular affinity for children, not having had a childhood to speak of himself. Royal duties took him into contact with them, but children were just one more foreign culture with whom certain rituals were observed. He didn't live among them or desire to.

What he did understand was that they were vulnerable. Those who exploited the weak were beneath contempt. Only a true monster would hurt someone as helpless as a nine-year-old girl, especially sexually.

"I didn't think I could get pregnant." Trella's thin voice echoed off the concrete and steel of his garage, underpinned by the drone of the fan. Her profile was pale and still, grayed by the half-light beyond the row of windows in the doors. "The damage he did was that bad. Do you understand what I'm saying? Because I don't want to get any more specific."

A twisted, anguished feeling struck his middle, clenching talons around his chest and squeezing his throat, pushing fear and helplessness to such heights inside him, it became a pressure he could barely withstand. He knew his heart was beating because it throbbed with painful pounds that rang in his ears, but he couldn't move or speak.

There were no words, no reactions, that fit this situation. Only a primal scream that would have no effect whatsoever. It wouldn't reverse the past, wouldn't erase her dark memories. He was at a complete loss.

"When I realized I was pregnant, I had to give the baby a chance. Even though the odds were against it. I've been expecting a miscarriage every single day. What was the point in telling you if I was only going to lose it? Even now, I'm terrified of becoming too attached in case something happens."

It was his. The knowledge crashed over him like a wave, bringing a sharp sting of heightened awareness to his whole body. It changed everything. His entire life, every decision and action, filtered in a blur through this lens of a new life they had created.

The cogs in his brain finally began turning, but with a rustiness that scraped at his detachment.

"So this is…delicate?" What if she lost it? For some reason, neat as that solution might sound, the idea appalled him. "Are you all right?" He should have asked these questions the minute he'd had her alone. "Has this put you into labor? Are you in pain?"

"No." She skimmed her hair out of her eyes and let herself relax into the seat of the car, hands settling over her bump. Her complexion was pale, but she sounded calm. "We're both quite healthy, all things considered. But I see a specialist in London and she wants me on bed rest for the third trimester. She was an intern in Spain when I was a child and knows everything I've been through. I'll let your doctor take my blood, but I'm not giving some stranger my medical history. He touches my arm. That's *it*."

He nodded, still trying to put the pieces together.

"I know I should have told you sooner, but I also knew that if I carried this baby to a stage where it could survive birth, then I would have to marry you. I don't want to."

Her gaze finally came up, striking into him like a harsh winter wind. Bleak.

"I thought if I ever married, it would be for love." Despondency pulled her brows together and her thick lashes swept down to hide her eyes again. "That makes me sound like a romantic and I'm not. I just don't want to be something taken on in sufferance. My sister fell in love. I know it's possible."

Her elbow came up to rest on the door and she set her teeth on her thumbnail.

"Plus, my life is already high profile. Yours is worse." Her hand dropped away and she flashed him a look of blame. "Why can't you be a mechanic or something? Your life comes with even more restrictions than I imposed on myself. Why would I sign up for that? Of course I avoided telling you."

He certainly wouldn't live this life if he had a choice, but it struck him as odd that she disparaged his station. Every other woman aspired to be his queen.

"So, yes, I've handled this badly. God knows I've been informed of *that* more than once." She rolled her eyes. "I probably owe you an apology."

"Probably?" Did she have any idea the damage she had caused by avoiding him?

"I'm not sorry. I will never be sorry that I'm trying to have our baby." Her chin came up, defiant and fierce, but with deep vulnerability edging her unblinking eyes.

Something stirred in him. Gratitude? How? This baby was a disaster.

As if she read his mind, the corners of her mouth went down. "And I think we'll do enough damage to each other in the next while that if we start apologizing now, we'll be peaking way too early."

*Never trust anyone who can't make or take a joke*, his father had told him once. *Your grandmother, for instance*, had been the rest of the crack.

His grandmother. Yes, indeed, there would be hell to pay and many, many apologies to make.

Before he could fully grasp the scope of impact, a dull buzz emanated from the front of her shirt. "Goodness, an hour gone already?" She reached inside her collar to bring her phone from her bra, voice shaken but trying for lighthearted. "*Hola*, Henri. I'm fine. Just congratulating the father of my child. Does he look green to you?"

Trella could ignore the signs for only so long. The nausea churning in her belly, the heart palpitations, the hot and cold sweats. An attack was upon her. Of course it was. This was one of the most stressful days of her life and she was doing everything wrong, making it worse. Maybe she *did* self-sabotage, the way her brother Ramon sometimes accused, but she would rather eat live worms than admit he was right about anything.

She hated to admit any sort of weakness, because she knew, deep down, that she *was* weak. There was no hiding it from her family, but few others knew exactly what a basket case she was. That's why she'd spent so many years sequestered in the family compound. It had provided the security and stability she'd needed to overcome the worst of her issues, but it had kept her pride intact, too.

Ridiculous pride that kept her from admitting she was falling apart to Xavier and his doctor.

Gunter took her blood then her blood pressure, which he noted was elevated. He frowned and began asking pointed questions about her pregnancy.

She clammed up. The truth was, she wasn't combative as a result of being kidnapped. She'd been born that way, much to her family's eternal frustration. Her experience only gave her an excuse for it.

At her silence, Xavier turned from the window where he'd been standing in quiet contemplation. "Pass the readings to her specialist. She can determine if further action is necessary and advise a treatment plan. Request her doctor come to Lirona as soon as possible and stay for the duration of the pregnancy."

"She has other patients," Trella pointed out.

"None so important as you," he stated with a humorless smile.

"Flatterer," she tried, but her own sense of humor was buried beneath an onslaught of sensory overload ticking toward detonation.

"Sir, I've performed many deliveries," the doctor argued. "There's no need—"

"Sweeten the deal however you must. Our women's health initiative is due for an upgrade, I'm sure. Expenses won't be spared."

"Very generous, sir," the royal physician said more firmly. "I'm sure many Elazarians would benefit, but..." He cleared his throat. "Perhaps such an undertaking should wait until DNA results are received."

"The results are for the Queen. I'm confident this is my heir. But I do have to inform her. *Bella*, please advise your brother we'll be on the move again, but not for long. The palace isn't far."

That was when she should have said, *I can't*.

She knew what kind of self-care was needed. A quiet, dark room. A sibling holding her hand, talking her down from her mental ledge.

She didn't say anything. Her stupid, tender pride, knocked to the ground so many times, locked her teeth while the rest of her began a slow collapse.

Now she sat in the back of his sedan, gripping her elbows as the ghouls came for her. It was going to be a bad one. She could taste it. The sheer frustration of not being able to stave it off made her eyes sting. Her mind spun down ever more scary avenues. Dark, harmful thoughts crowded in, feeding the anxiety.

*This is my life now.*

There would be no escape from the attention. It would be worse. Harsher. More judgmental. All the things she had tried to avoid by keeping her pregnancy secret and withholding the father's name were going to come true now.

The pressure in her chest grew worse, suffocating her, and even though her specialist had assured her from the beginning that suffering an attack wouldn't hurt the baby, she was convinced it would, *knew it*. She was going to lose her baby because she couldn't control these awful spells.

While Xavier watched her lose *everything*. He would reject her for being the disaster she was. Even if she managed to keep his baby and deliver it some weeks from now, he would take it from her. He might have her locked away.

*She needed Gili.* She took out her phone and gripped it so hard her hand ached. Where were Henri and Ramon? They wouldn't let anyone take her baby. They would always keep her safe.

*No.* She couldn't keep expecting them to turn up and save her from herself.

"Why are you breathing like that? Are you asthmatic?"

She shook her head and turned her face to the window, wanting to die because now he'd noticed she was off and was staring at her.

"I'll ask Gunter if he reached your doctor." He started to lean forward.

She grabbed his sleeve. "Don't."

"You're flushed." He touched the backs of his fingers to her cheek then her forehead, making her flinch. "Sweating."

"It's nothing," she lied in a strangled voice, and was both relieved and horrified that her phone began to ripple with the heavenly notes of a harp.

It took two tries to open the call. When her sister appeared, she wasn't in focus. Tears of homesickness and failure filled her eyes. "Gili."

"I know, *bella*," she sounded equally anxious. "I can feel it. Where are you? Still at the Prince's chalet?"

"I don't know." The realization that she was in a strange land had been stalking her. Admitting it made it real and added to her terror. Her heart was so tight, she feared it was going into arrest. She clutched at the front of her shirt. "We're driving. How will you find me if we're moving? I'm so scared, Gili."

"I know, *fillette*. Breathe. Count your oranges. I'm coming. See, I'm going through the door. Henri has been tracking you all day. We'll always find you, you know that. Are you still with the Prince?"

Trella looked up and saw Xavier staring at her like her hair was made of snakes.

It was the most humiliating moment of her life. She couldn't make it worse by having her sister come to her like she was a child. *Couldn't.*

"No." She turned back to her phone. "You're married now. You have to stay with Kasim."

"He understands. I've already sent someone to tell him and prepare the helicopter."

It sounded so outlandish. What other person had family flying in from all corners to save her from imaginary threats?

"No, Gili." She managed to sound firm, even though turning away her sister felt like plunging a knife into her own chest. "I don't want you to come. I mean it."

"*Bella*," her sister breathed as though she'd felt the knife, too, in the back.

"I have to learn, Gili. I *have* to. I'm going to hang up and I'll call you later—"

"Wait! Let me speak to the Prince. He needs to understand."

Since there was no way Trella could explain it herself, she pushed the phone toward him.

"It's a panic attack," Gili said. "She doesn't need drugs or a hospital or strangers making her relive why this is happening. She needs to feel safe. Is there a hotel where you can secure a room? I don't mean book one. I mean *secure* it."

"We'll be at the palace in ten minutes."

"Good. Get her into a quiet bedroom, keep the lights low, blinds down, guards at the door. She needs to let it run its course without fearing people are going to see her. Keep her warm and whatever she says, remind her she's safe. If you can't stay with her, I'll come."

"I'll stay with her." His voice was grim. He handed back the phone.

She ended the call, mortified by how needy her sister had made her sound. Appalled because it was true. She hadn't tried to weather a spell on her own since they had first started. It had been a disaster.

Nevertheless, she screwed up her courage, pressed the phone between her breasts, and spoke some of the hardest words that had ever passed her lips. "You don't have to babysit me."

She held her breath, dreading the prospect of going it alone.

"I'm not letting you out of my sight until that baby is born."

The harsh words jarred, taking her brief flash of gratitude and coating it in foreboding.

# CHAPTER SIX

XAVIER HAD THE car drive to the postern gate, where delivery trucks and other utility vehicles came in. They took a lane through the back garden to the private apartments. It was a longer, slower, but much more discreet entrance into the palace built by a king three hundred years ago.

Did coming in this way also allow him to avoid Mario and any mention of his grandmother's expectation that he present himself? A man did what he had to for the mother of his unborn child.

Xavier didn't *do* emotion. Fits and tempers were signs of poor breeding. He'd been taught that from an early age. When women became histrionic, he offered space.

Not possible today. And as much as he wanted to hold himself apart from the way Trella was behaving, he couldn't. She was shaking, hair damp at her temples, eyes darting. When he helped her from the car, she clung to his sleeve and looked to every shadow.

It was unnerving. Even stranger, her sense of threat put him on guard.

He kept reminding himself this was a panic attack, something he knew very little about except that it was a false response. Nevertheless, her fear provoked a very real primal need in him to offer protection. His heart pounded with readiness and he scanned about as they moved, fingers twitching for a weapon. He'd never experienced such an atavistic, bloodthirsty reaction. He was not so far removed from his medieval ancestors as he had imagined. He was completely prepared to shed his cloak of civility and slay if necessary.

Staff leapt to their feet as they walked through the kitchen. He said nothing, only pulled her into the service elevator.

Gunter came with them, frowning as he saw how distraught she looked. "Are you in pain?" He tried to take her pulse.

Trella shrank into Xavier.

"Leave her alone." He closed his arms around her. Her firm bump nudged low on his abdomen, reminding him that her panic attack was only the tip of the iceberg where this confounding day was concerned.

His valet, Vincente, met them as they entered his apartment. Xavier had moved into his father's half of the rooms when he'd finished university and never even glanced toward the adjoined feminine side, but it was kept dusted for the ghosts of past queens.

He pressed Trella toward the canopied bed of gold and red then started to close the doors, telling Vincente, "I'm locking us in. Leave sandwiches in my lounge. If I need anything else, I'll text. No one comes in here. *No one.*"

"Of course, sir." He read Vincente's apprehension. "But I believe the Queen—"

"Inform her I'll be along when I can, but it will be some time."

Xavier did as he'd promised, moving to lock each door and close all the drapes, turning on one bedside lamp as he went. Then he shook out a soft blanket from a chest and brought it to where Trella sat on the edge of the bed.

She clutched the blanket around her, back hunched, still trembling.

All he could see was a nine-year-old girl. Was this what that experience had left her with? He had a thousand questions, but heeded her sister's advice and only said, "You're safe, *bella*. This is my world. Nothing can harm you here."

Tears tracked her cheeks and she swiped the back of her hand along her jaw, skimming away the drips.

"I didn't want you to see me like this." Her voice was thin as a silk thread. "I wanted you to think I was Gili. She cries at proper things, like weddings and stubbed toes. She's afraid of real things, not stuff she makes up in her head."

Was it made-up? He used the satin on the corner of the blanket to dry her cheeks, not sure where the urge to comfort came from. It wasn't taught or ingrained. Manners and platitudes got him through displays like this, not affection.

But he felt responsible for her and her attack. "I only wanted to talk to you. I didn't expect things to go off the rails like this."

"Don't blame yourself. I take everything further than it needs to go." She drew in a shaken sigh. Her eyes filled again.

"Is this what you were hiding, staying out of the spotlight all those years?"

She nodded jerkily. "It started after Papa died. We were fifteen. I was starting to feel like I might be able to go back to school and have a normal life. But we were seen as sex objects, I guess, because the most disgusting men found us online. I'd already been through an eating disorder and trolls mocking me for it. Then all these men started sending photos and telling me what they wanted to do to me. It hit a switch."

A streak of impotent fury lodged in his chest. His entire life, he had struggled against this particular irony. He was a future monarch, charged with great power and responsibility, godlike in some eyes, but he couldn't control how people treated each other. He couldn't prevent the kind of harm that had Trella drawing up her knees so she was a ball of misery. His inability to help her struck at the deepest part of him.

"I'm a woman of extremes. You might as well know that about me. Give me that pillow."

He dragged it closer and she fell onto her side and buried her face in it. She sobbed so deeply, was in the throes of an anguish so terrible, he was stricken witnessing it. How did she withstand it?

*Let it run its course,* her sister had said. That seemed cruel.

He settled on the bed behind her, rubbed her arm and soothed her shaking back. It took several minutes for her crying to subside. She lifted her head and breathed as though she'd been running for miles.

"I keep worrying I'll have an attack while I'm in labor. My doctor says this won't hurt the baby, but I'm so scared all this adrenaline is causing damage. What if we go through all of this and our child isn't fit to reign? What if that's my fault because I can't control this?"

"Is there nothing you can take? Something safe during pregnancy?"

"No. I mean, maybe, but I can't. *Won't.*" She threw her arm over her eyes. "I tried drugs years ago. They made me depressed and dependent. I was close to taking a whole bottle just to end this."

She dropped her arm and twisted to stare at him from between matted lashes.

"I shouldn't have told you that. You'll declare me unfit and take our baby away. Oh, God..."

She rolled around the pillow again, dragging the blanket with her and pulling it over her head.

"Trella." He was no mental health expert, but he knew a tailspin when he heard one. He settled on the mattress behind her, propped on an elbow, letting his body heat penetrate the blanket as he gave rubs of reassurance against her shoulder and arm. He wanted to fold right around her, absorb whatever had such a terrible grip on her.

"Let's take this one thing at a time. Hmm? The baby is well. Your doctor said so, yes? Do you know the sex?"

It took a minute, but her breathing settled to something more natural.

"I've been afraid to ask, thinking it would make me more attached. I'm so scared I'm going to lose it." She shifted, pushing away the blanket to reveal her face, then peeled the blanket all the way back, piling it on him as she exposed her bump. She smoothed her shirt over the roundness. "It's moving. Do you want to feel?"

He stalled, reality hitting him like a train. He let her draw his hand across the tense swell of her midsection. He had thought it would feel like an inflated beach ball, but she was warm and there was give within the firmness. A shape. Something that felt no bigger than his knuckle pressed outward, moving across the palm of his hand.

He almost jerked back, yet he was too fascinated and kept his hand in place, waiting to feel it again. "Does that hurt?"

"It reassures me. *Hola, bebé. Cómo estás?*"

Another tiny kick struck his hand, prompting a soft noise of amusement deep in her throat. She turned her head to look at him. Her eyelids were red and swollen, but her smile was so filled with joy and wonder, she took his breath away.

The moment snaked out like a rope to encircle and draw them together, binding them, inexorable and eternal.

He sucked in a breath, drawing back as he tried to pull himself free of what threatened to carry him into deep waters like a deadly riptide.

"How are we even here? How—Why me, *bella?*"

"Why did I sleep with you? I didn't plan to sleep with anyone." She curled around her pillow, rubbing her face against it, drying tears. "I only wanted to practice being in public. I was so proud for having the courage to talk to a man, then to be alone with one. You made me feel normal. Safe. I needed that. I was using you. I admit that. But sleeping with you?" She craned her neck to look at him, her expression helpless. Anxious. "I couldn't help myself. You said we were volatile. That…"

He knew what he had said. It had been true. He'd never experienced anything like what he'd felt with her that night. Despite his best efforts, the memory haunted him. He wasn't a dependent person, but he was disturbingly gratified to be this close to her again. The animal inside him had finally stopped pacing with restless frustration.

He was loath to admit any of that, though. Her power to still affect him unnerved him. "It was my last night before I got engaged. We were both attributing significance for our own reasons."

The light in her eyes dimmed with hurt. She withdrew, turning away again.

He closed his fist in the tangle of blanket across their hips, lungs turning to lead.

"Either way, it gave me hope that I could *be* normal. Maybe fall in love and get married, someday. That's all I've ever wanted. To be normal. Now I never will be, because I'm carrying a royal baby and I was so happy to be pregnant, but I knew this was a disaster. You have your life and I've never had any life at all. I deserve a chance to be single and free. Free of *this*!"

Her tension returned in a contraction of her muscles that drew her in like a shrinking bloom, fists coming up to her clenched eyes.

"I told Gili I would run Maison des Jumeaux. When we were little, she was able to count on me. I want to be that person people can rely on, but I'm always going to be this pathetic—"

"Trella. You *have* to stop escalating."

"Do you think I can control it?" Her hands went into her hair, clenching handfuls. "I try. I really try, but the fear *grips* me. Now we have to get married and you don't want some crazy burden of a wife. You'll hate me. I'm *so scared* of what will happen."

"Stop." He couldn't stand it. He pressed his body heat around her, held her in sheltering arms and willed her back to calm. "Hatred is a wasted emotion. It closes all pathways to resolving a conflict. Our situation is difficult, but hating each other won't make it easier."

Her trembling continued, but he felt the moment his words penetrated. Her hands loosened in her hair.

"That sounds very wise," she said on a sniff. "Do they teach you that in monarchy school?"

"Divorce class. My mother was a great believer in practical demonstrations."

She unfolded a few increments more. "When we were in Paris, you said your mother was sent away by your grandmother because she wanted a divorce?"

He eased his embrace, regretting his loose lips. He had learned out of necessity to be comfortable with his own thoughts, never needing confidantes, but keeping her mind engaged seemed to forestall her emotional downtrends, so he answered.

"She made a commitment then didn't accept her lot. Unhappy wives move into the dowager wing. They don't reject royal life altogether. My mother tried separation, but my father and grandmother pressured her to have another baby. Since their marriage was over, she refused. She was granted a divorce on the grounds that she left Elazar. She had family in Germany so she moved there."

"Exiled, you said. But you still saw her? How old were you?" She tried to twist enough to see him.

He used the weight of his arm to keep them spooned. Her hair tickled his lips while the scent of her went straight to the back of his brain, finding where she had imprinted herself in Paris and settling like a puzzle piece matched to its empty space.

He shook off the notion. "I was eight. At

boarding school. My life wasn't affected much. We exchanged a few letters, but what was there to say?"

"You didn't see her *at all*?" She tried harder to twist, rolling onto her back and forcing him to meet her gaze. "Do you see her now?"

"We send Christmas cards." He shrugged off the jabs of rejection that still came alive when he revisited the memory. "Chosen by our personal assistants. We're not sentimental people."

Her expression grew appalled. "What about your father? You said you were young when he abdicated?"

"Renounced," he corrected, regretting this. It was becoming too intimate. Too uncomfortable.

"Do you see him?"

"It was best we didn't communicate." *This* communication ended here, he conveyed by drawing back.

"But—" She groaned and rolled to face him fully. He could see a fresh wave of emotion taking its grip on her. Her hand closed on the front of his shirt, catching at a few chest hairs, making him wince. "Now I'm worried you'll drop out of our child's life like that. Swear to me you won't."

He covered her hand, loosening her fist and holding her slender fingers. He had to consciously overcome an urge to draw her hand to his mouth and kiss her bruised knuckles, even as he acknowledged she was far more likely to disappear than he was. Royal life was not easy, especially when shoved to the fringes as his mother had been. He didn't blame his mother for extricating herself, and wouldn't censure Trella when she did it, especially if the stress of life in the public eye put her in paroxysms like this.

"Duty may have skipped a generation, but it is firmly drilled into me. I will never forsake my obligation to our child."

"Obligation." Her brow furrowed. "What about love?"

He dried her cheek with his thumb. "Love is a problem not a solution."

"Who told you *that*?"

"It's an observation. My mother loved my father, which is why she couldn't bear his cheating. My father loved the woman who cost him his kingdom. Duty is more reliable."

She shook her head.

"I don't have to argue with you, *bella*. Time reveals all. Now, let's stop talking about things that upset you. What did your sister say about counting oranges? Tell me why she said that."

Xavier hadn't had his backside handed to him on one of the palace's sixteenth-century gold platters since his teen years. He refused to allow it today.

He had had plenty of time in the night, lying awake making decisions between comforting Trella through crying spells and nightmares, until she fell deeply asleep in the early hours.

He rose to put his plans into action and by the time the Queen summoned him, he was able to preempt a shredding of his character by proving what he had told Trella—he adhered to duty above all else.

"She has agreed to that?"

"She will."

"And you?"

"Of course. Why wouldn't I?"

The Queen cocked a skeptical brow. "You spent last night with her. That implies…preoccupation."

"You think we were having sex? No." Despite having few secrets from his grandmother, her intrusive remark grated. "She was upset."

"Gunter said she's fragile." Her mouth pursed with disdain. Ruling required strength of every kind, especially emotional.

He frowned, annoyed that Gunter's report had preceded his own, especially because it was off the mark. Trella was besieged. It was different.

"She held off telling me because her pregnancy is high-risk."

"So, it would seem, is she."

An urge to defend her stayed lodged in his

throat. She *was* a threat—one he was mitigating to the best of his ability.

"When would you like to meet her?" he asked instead.

"Perhaps after the baby is born?"

He hadn't slept. That's why the snub struck him as unconscionably rude.

Before he could react, Mario entered. "Deepest apologies, your Majesty, but Ms. Sauveterre's brother insists on seeing her. We've stalled him as long as possible."

"He's *here*?" Xavier's heart lurched with protectiveness and a jolt of alarm. Trella was catching up on much-needed sleep. More importantly, "We both spoke to him yesterday. She told him she was staying for the foreseeable future."

*She couldn't leave.*

"I believe it's the race-car driver. She has agreed to receive him. I thought you would wish to—"

"I would." Xavier strode from the room. When he heard raised voices as he approached the apartment they now shared, his aggression increased. With a snap of his fingers, security personnel fell into step behind him. He pushed into what had once been his mother's parlor.

Trella was red-faced as she confronted a man who looked like Henri but emanated a hot-tempered demeanor that was in complete contrast to his brother's air of aloof control. "No, *you* shut up—" Ramon was saying to his sister.

"Leave quietly or I'll have you removed." Xavier would do it himself. He was in that kind of mood.

Ramon snorted as he gave Xavier a measuring once-over, hands on his hips, looking willing for the fight Xavier promised.

"Don't." Trella threw herself against her brother's side, looping her arms tight around his waist. "I was saying things he didn't want to hear."

Despite the animosity that had been flaring between them seconds before, Ramon curled a shielding arm around his sister, even as he frowned at her, concern evident beneath his glare of impatience.

Trella looked as rough as the night she'd had. When Xavier had left her, she'd been subdued and exhausted, falling back asleep within seconds after he'd woken her to tell her he was leaving. She still had dark circles under red eyes and hadn't changed out of the silk pajamas he'd given her to wear to bed. In fact, she'd raided his closet for a thick cardigan to belt over them.

Xavier snapped out of searching her expression to realize she was bickering with her brother, refusing to go with him.

"All those times you showed up when I called makes it possible for me to work through this.

I know you *will* come if I ask. That means everything. But until I ask, you *have* to *butt out*."

With a resigned scowl, Ramon dropped his arm from around her. "*Bueno.*"

"And be nicer to Iz—"

"No. Butting out goes both ways. And you *will* introduce me to your host."

"Did you call me a *virgin*?" Xavier asked Trella in an ominous tone as they entered his suite hours later. "You switched between French and Spanish so often, I might have heard wrong."

She tried not to snicker. "I told you it was a bad habit. Ramon and I are the worst because we get heated and grab the first word that comes in any language."

Ramon had joined them for a meal that might have been pleasant if so many questions hadn't been hanging over her like a guillotine blade. If he'd caught her alone again, he would have skewered her with all of them, she was sure, but he'd behaved. They had played verbal tennis as they always did, sticking to neutral topics like films and current events.

Sparring with her brother always helped restore her confidence. Where Gili was her security blanket and Henri was her rock, Ramon was her worthy adversary, keeping her sharp and forcing her to hold her own. She was tired and stifling yawns, but her lingering melancholy had lightened. As she looked into the cloudy crystal ball that was her future, she was thinking, *I can do this*.

Especially because, like her, Xavier seemed to be experiencing the same threads of attraction they'd felt when they had made this baby. A selection from her closet in Paris had arrived earlier and she now wore a dark blue skirt and a white maternity top. It draped her breasts in such a flattering way, she'd caught Xavier eyeing her chest more than once while they ate, making her tingle and giving her hope.

She turned her back on him and lifted her hair, silently requesting he release the tiny clasp at the top of her spine, realizing she hadn't properly answered his question. "And yes, I did. Ramon asked me how you did with looking after me through my attack. I said pretty well, for a virgin."

"Lovely. I hope the dining staff enjoyed that." His breath warmed the back of her neck along with the light brush of his fingertips, making her shiver.

"I said worse. I called Ramon a—"

"I heard that one. Very clearly," he cut in dryly, motioning her to lead the way to her side of the apartment. "Because of his engagement to 'Izzy.'"

"Isidora, yes. She's a dear friend. Her father handled our media for years. Aside from Gili, she was my *only* friend for a long time."

Her heart dipped and rolled when he turned, locking them into her bedroom. Despite her rough night, sleeping with him had been more than comforting. She had liked the brushes of contact and the inherent intimacy, the way his strong arms had made her feel so safe. It had given her that bonding feeling she had felt in Paris, one that was incredibly bolstering.

His efforts to comfort also gave her hope for their marriage. All her flaws had been laid bare, yet he had stayed with her. She was deeply gratified. Touched.

Now all she had to explain was that, as much as she might like to, she couldn't make love. Practically blushing at the mere thought, because she was so deeply tempted, she moved to take up her brush and began working it through her hair, trying to act casual as nerves accosted her.

He moved to lean on the footboard of the bed, appearing in the mirror behind her. The way he watched as she stroked her hair made her feel as though she was enticing him. The crackle of tension on the air was exciting, giving her that sense of power in her sexuality he'd instilled the first time. Oh, she wished their timing wasn't so far off.

His expression tightened before he jerked his gaze away, clearing his throat. "If she's such a good friend, why don't you approve of her?"

"Who? Oh. Um." She blushed at having her mind fixated on intimate acts while he was clearly not. "I approve of Isidora completely, but Ramon is sleeping with her."

"Stickler for waiting until after the wedding, are you?" He dropped a pointed gaze to her middle.

"Ha-ha." She tapped the brush against her thigh then set it aside. "No, their engagement is a publicity stunt. Earlier this year, Isidora took over her father's position at Sauveterre International." Trella took off her earrings and bracelet. "You'll notice Ramon's very public proposal coincides with the first photos of my pregnancy showing up online. He does that all the time, takes the spotlight off the rest of us. Izzy is so loyal she went along with it, but she had a terrific crush on Ramon when we were young. He never returned it and shouldn't sleep with her if he has no intention of marrying her. She's going to get hurt. That makes me mad."

"I see. Well, kindly convey that we would prefer fewer stunts in future. My team will handle—" he indicated her middle again "—this."

She blinked, not expecting him to be worried for Izzy, not really, but his cool attention to his own interests sent a premonition down her spine like a drip of icy water.

It occurred to her that he had closed the door not because he wanted to nurture the growing trust between them. He wanted to have a conversation that was best held within the gilded cage he'd assigned her.

Logically she knew she had imprinted on her first lover like a baby duckling emerging from its protective shell. She'd spent weeks reliving Paris and imagining this reunion, dreaming up scenarios where he was as happy about her pregnancy as she was.

It was delusional. She had known that, but apparently she was still building castles in the sky because a minute ago, she had been okay with his knowing all her worst secrets. Now a grossly naked sensation accosted her, like he had leverage on her.

She tried to disguise her apprehension with a tough smile. "It's time to discuss *this*. Isn't it?"

The barest flicker of emotion reflected in his blink. He folded his arms and tilted his head in assent. "Gunter informs me your doctor has accepted my offer of a residency at Hospital del Re, with a mandate to ensure our obstetrics wing is the best in the world. She'll be here tomorrow and has requested a private room be prepared for you."

"Bed rest." Trella had known it was coming, but still made a face of dismay.

"You'll fight it?"

"No." She wasn't able to keep the dread from her voice, though. "It's for the best."

"It is."

Something in his tone, in the subtle shift of his expression, pricked up her ears. Relief? His approval of her going into the hospital had nothing to do with the health of their unborn child. He was protecting his own interests again!

An ache of hurt spread through her until all her sweet imaginings had been pushed out and she was left with the ugly reality. She really had been deceiving herself all these months.

"Keeps me out of sight, does it? Is that the Queen's preference? Or yours?" Behind the stir of their child, her abdomen tightened.

His expression grew even more shuttered. "It's expedient for all. You said you don't want the attention our association brings."

"Don't pretend you're doing me a favor. Are we not marrying, then?" Clearly not, if he was hiding her away.

Her arms pulled into a defensive fold across her front. Her shoulders grew rock hard while she ignored the creep of anguish that began working in tendrils through her core. What did she care? She didn't want a husband anyway!

Right?

"Of course we'll marry." He mirrored her posture, arms folded, seeming relaxed in the way he leaned on the footboard, but there was a stillness to him, an implacability in his tone. "Elazar had a bastard monarch in the 1700s. It was a bloody fight to keep the reign. We've been sticklers for legitimacy ever since."

She understood she was speaking to a future king now, not the charming prince who had lulled her with something that had resembled caring. Twice.

"Our marriage will be a private ceremony. Announced, but without fanfare. No formal photos. We'll keep it brief."

"The ceremony? Or the marriage?"

"Both."

The tendons in her neck flexed as she fought a choke, doing her best to hide how deeply he was striking against her hard-won self-worth. "How brief?"

"We'll divorce by the end of the year."

Her teeth closed on the inside of her lip, biting down harder and harder until she had to consciously remind herself not to break the skin.

What had she expected after showing him her true colors? A declaration of love? A desire to live out his life with *that*? Well, she knew exactly how much *duty* he felt toward her, didn't she? Not even four months' worth.

"That's quite the virgin birth you're orchestrating."

His eyes narrowed at her shaken tone. "Is this conversation going to bring on another attack?"

Oh, she hated above all things to be managed like she was too delicate for honesty.

"I do better when I know what's coming." Her voice only trembled a little, mostly from the effort to hide the burn of disgrace sizzling under her skin. "Is this room a time machine, by the way? I feel we've gone back to your 1700s and I'm something shameful you're sweeping under the rug."

"It isn't about hiding you." He showed the barest hint of discomfort by dropping his hands to the footboard and pushing to stand. "I'm acknowledging you and the heir you're providing me, but it would be helpful if your role was downplayed, so as not to overshadow Patrizia's."

"You're still *engaged*?"

"It's been called off, since I'm marrying you, but—"

"She's still willing to marry you?" The news pushed her into falling back a step. Maybe it was the realization that he still wanted that marriage himself. Why did that hurt? So much?

"Unless a better offer comes along, she is not

averse to reviving our plan after you and I divorce." He must have read the incredulity in her expression, because he said, "We're friends. Both ruled by duty. The fact we *don't* have strong feelings for each other and she's *not* hurt by this—" again with the generic wave at her middle "—is the reason we're a good fit."

"But her child won't be first in line! Or is she hoping mine's a girl?"

"Gender isn't an issue in Elazar. First born is first in line, but..." He seemed to debate whether she could handle his next words before he said, without emotion, "Until you deliver a healthy baby, many aspects of this situation remain fluid."

Trella sucked in a gasp so sharp it went down the back of her throat like a spear, sticking in her heart and pinning her motionless. She tried telling herself the shivery clamp around her was anger, but it was anguish. Dark, blood-red betrayal.

"How *dare* you give someone *hope* that I'll lose our baby."

"It's not hope." He strode away from the foot of the bed in a sudden rush, making her jerk back another step and keep him in her line of sight. "It's caution. You said this will be your only pregnancy. There is a reason for an heir and a spare. If my uncle had lived, this conversation wouldn't even be happening. If my mother had done her duty, I would have other choices. I don't. I will accept what comes of this pregnancy, but I have to ensure there are alternatives."

She was so appalled that she wasn't even sure what the cold feeling against her lips was. Her fingers? All of her felt cold and empty and deeply furious.

She barely tracked that his hand flicked the air. Through her own haze of emotion, she had a brief impression of bitterness before he turned his back on her.

Anything close to suffering on his part was imagined, though. Had to be. Everything she had shared with this man was imagination and faulty memory. A wish. Girlish daydreaming. A rescue fantasy.

He was a spoiled prince who had sullied a maiden and was tidying up that mess the most pragmatic way possible.

"This really is medieval times, isn't it? Women have come all this way, yet I'm still just a vessel. A faulty one." She knew she was broken. It shouldn't surprise her that she was being rejected. She had thought she had prepared herself, but she hadn't. She was gutted and had to fight with everything in her not to reveal how devastated she was.

So many times, she'd wished she could go back to that moment as an impetuous girl, when Gili's math tutor had called out to her. She had run to tell him he had the wrong twin, *that's all*. It had been one second of impulse and she was still being punished for it.

Xavier's head tipped back as he aimed his gaze at the portrait of an ancestor surveying them from high on the wall.

"If I don't produce our next ruler, the crown passes to a family living in America for the last two hundred years. Rather than let that happen, our neighbors would squabble to take control of Elazar. Instability would ripple across Europe. The globe. We're a small country, but a pivotal one. I need more than one child to ensure Elazar's future. I need a wife with connections that cement our alliances."

His voice held not one iota of regret or even concern for how his plan would affect *this* child. Or her.

"Spell it out for me." She grappled for her most pragmatic tone. "Exactly how is this to work? Because I am not allowing some strange woman to raise my baby."

"Our child will be raised by nannies, tutors and servants, same as you and I."

"*I* wasn't!"

"You left for boarding school at *seven*. If you

hadn't been kidnapped, you would have grown up there. Your brothers did."

"My parents traveled, but they were very involved. We knew they loved us!"

As she stared into his half-lidded eyes and read indifference, it struck her why he was being so dispassionate rather than weighing his decisions through his heart.

"You don't know what that's like, do you?" She felt cruel saying it, but everything he had told her about his parents came back to her, bringing his brutally logical plan into focus.

His brow went up in arrogant query. "What?"

"Love."

He might have flinched, but it was gone so fast that she wasn't sure. His sigh was pure condescension as he pushed his hands into his pockets. "I told you last night—"

"I'm not talking about romantic love. *Family* love."

"Love of any kind isn't real." His voice slapped her down for being so gullible. "Look around. Is it here? Keeping anyone in my life but my grandmother? Loyalty. Obligation. Duty. Those are real."

She would have argued that her family loved her, but something else struck with brutal force. "Are you saying—"

She had a flash of her mother crying with joy

because Trella was pregnant. Elisa Sauveterre was worried sick and had strong opinions on how Trella had avoided telling Xavier, but beneath all of that was pure, over-the-moon love for her unborn grandchild.

"Is your grandmother happy we're having a baby?" Her voice quavered with strain.

His jaw set. "That is not the word I would use, no."

"Wow." A jagged laugh clawed inside her chest. "Just wow." How did one survive such an emotional desert?

The answer was before her. They turned into this—an image of a man with a heart, but one who was actually incapable of deeper feelings. One who scoffed at love.

A fierce gleam—torment?—flashed in his gaze before he steeled himself behind a visage of hammered armor. "But she recognizes we have a responsibility toward it."

"Precious obligation," she said shakily. "Here's some news for you. I will *not* be shut out of my child's life and replaced by nannies and tutors. I'll call in the rescue team right now and barricade us in Sus Brazos for the rest of our lives if that's what you're thinking."

"Dramatics will not be necessary," he said with pithy disdain. "We'll share custody, fifty-fifty. Aside from security and education, how you meet the needs of our child is your business. Visitations to Spain or elsewhere can be worked out as they arise. But our child lives in Elazar." He pointed at the floor. "I will provide you with a home here in Lirona as part of our divorce settlement."

She shouldn't care how quickly he got rid of her. He was being so cold, acting so far removed from the man she had wanted to believe he was, she could hardly endure facing the next minute in his company let alone four months of marriage.

It still took effort to say, "Well, that's a relief." She held his gaze, saying goodbye to those moments when he had held her and touched her as if there had been more between them than obligation. "I can move on then, too."

His eyes narrowed with warning, gaze so hard and devoid of feeling she struggled to hold the contact. "You can."

How foolish of her to try getting under his skin. She looked away, thinking that she couldn't stay this close to him with her defenses annihilated the way they were.

"Where is this dowager wing of which you spoke?"

"You'll sleep where I can keep an eye on you. You were difficult enough to track down as it was."

"Confinement. How apropos. And *familiar*."

"I won't apologize. We've agreed it's wasted."

"I still won't forgive you."

"Because I'm not upending my life?"

"Because you don't want our baby!"

"I don't want our *situation*."

*You don't want me!* She didn't say it. She was appalled she had thought it and turned her face away, boiling in humiliation. Pressure filled her throat and sat livid behind her eyes.

Into the thick silence, he sighed. "What I want has never mattered, *bella*. Duty to the crown takes precedence. I learned that a long time ago."

His voice was surprisingly gentle, which made the lash of the words all the more cutting and intolerable.

"Don't call me that. It's a family nickname and implies we're closer than we are, but it's just something you say when you can't remember the name of the woman you're sleeping with."

Another loaded silence filled the room like an acrid cloud.

"Explain to me how sniping at each other will make this easier."

"It's the *truth*." She swallowed past the ache in her throat, but it only lodged deeper in her chest. "You called me that in Paris and it made me think you saw *me*, not my sister, but all you saw was a willing partner. I need to stop thinking we're friends. Stop acting like we are."

They were still strangers and would remain so. He kept his heart behind thicker walls than she had ever hidden behind.

"If you insist. Trella."

"Thank you." She wasn't grateful. She was shattered. "Can you—" She waved at the door. "I'm tired."

"Will you be all right alone?"

She had thought he couldn't hurt her any further, but that did it. After rejecting her so roundly, did he really think she would want to cling to *him* through another emotional storm? How did he manage to sound like he *cared* if she suffered alone?

"I have to learn to be, don't I? I've known that for a long time. Goodnight."

# CHAPTER SEVEN

*I NEED TO stop thinking we're friends.*

There was no reason he should have lost sleep over that. Perhaps the *bella* endearment *had* always rolled off his tongue very easily around women, but for some reason knowing it held a more intimate connotation for her made it something he wanted the right to use. He doubted he would ever use it again with anyone else. It was hers now, which made it doubly frustrating she refused to hear it from him.

He went into his first meeting of the day, unrested and gritty eyed, only to face the woman still torturing him. They were about to negotiate their prenuptial agreement.

He introduced her to the palace attorney who fell under her spell at the first flash of her smile. She wore a pin-striped sky blue jacket over a white shirt that draped untucked over her matching skirt. It made her look smart and capable, yet sensual. Achingly vulnerable.

"I should have invited your brother to stay for this," he said as he directed her into a comfortable armchair.

"Why?" She cooled when he touched her arm and delicately removed her elbow from his loose touch, adjusting a cushion behind her back as she sat.

"To protect your interests."

"You can email the draft to him," the attorney said with a magnanimous smile. "If he has concerns, we can address them before you sign."

She sat back and folded her hands on her lap, smiling in a way that could only be called patronizing.

"Gentlemen. Along with our mother, my siblings and I jointly own Sauveterre International. Ramon votes Gili's share and Henri votes Mama's because they don't take an interest. I vote my own, thank you very much. Maison Des Jumeaux is not the only enterprise I've asked SI to underwrite. One hundred percent of my initiatives have turned a profit because I have a brain and use it. So…" She cut a glance toward Xavier. "The Prince may show the draft to his grandmother before *he* signs, to ensure *his* interests are protected, but I'm confident I can look after my own."

The attorney cleared his throat and shuffled papers.

Xavier held her lofty stare.

He should have been affronted. It was a well-executed burn in front of the attorney and his PA, but he was darkly thankful for that scorn in her.

He had watched her all through their meal with her brother yesterday, captivated by her rallying spirit. The glimpse of her family dynamic and the new facets in her personality had only made him want to know her far better than he would be allowed to. It had taken genuine effort on his part to stick to the plan and outline how they would proceed. If he had had a choice—

He didn't. So he had said what needed to be said.

She'd been angry. Injured. She *was* sentimental. And despite his claims to be anything but, he didn't take pleasure in hurting others. If things were different...

Wistfulness was a useless emotion. He steeled himself against futile *if only*s. "Let's get started."

As promised, Trella protected her abundant interests with pointed questions and clear language. The details were hammered out with very little fuss until the attorney asked, "And the dissolution of the marriage? Midnight, December thirty-first?"

"That's fine. But if I lose the baby, the marriage ends immediately."

Her statement was jarring. Xavier swung his head to regard her, disturbed.

"There would be no reason to draw it out," she said stiffly. White tension ringed her mouth.

A strange void opened in him. Why? She was right. What else was there between them besides the baby?

*You don't know what that's like, do you?*

Her disturbing accusation last night kept ambushing him, but his parents had been disruptive forces in his life, dividing his loyalty, creating nothing but turmoil and disappointment. If that was love, he didn't need it.

His grandmother's levelheaded reason and clear outline of what was expected from a future monarch had been a welcomed relief. Taking responsibility meant taking control.

Like love, Trella was an unpredictable influence. Too much was at stake to indulge any latent desires for either. She was right. Without the baby, they had nothing holding them in their union.

He lifted a finger, indicating the attorney should record that their marriage would end if the pregnancy did. He ignored the grate in the pit of his stomach.

They signed the contract a few days later, once the DNA results had been confirmed. Afterward, Trella hurried to greet her mother, who had arrived for the ceremony that would be held in the palace chapel.

"We agreed on a private ceremony," Xavier said when she informed him her mother would attend.

"She's giving me away." Trella hadn't mentioned her sister had cried over missing the ceremony. "All of my family wanted to be here, but neither of us is getting the wedding we wanted, are we? Well, I guess you are. Later."

His expression had hardened as he looked away.

She wasn't trying to be "combative," just stating fact. She had hoped she and Xavier would have something to build a family upon, but they didn't.

That made her sad, but all her soul-searching had been done in the months of keeping her pregnancy under wraps. Xavier had given her a chance at motherhood that she had believed was out of reach. For that, she would always be grateful.

But he saw her as, at best, one of the many staff who would tend to his offspring so he wouldn't have to. They might marry, but she wouldn't be his wife.

He didn't want *her*.

She had to ignore how spurned that made

her feel. She already had people who loved her, after all.

"*Mi niña hermosa*," her mother exclaimed as she finished buttoning the gown and Trella turned to face her. "Truly, this is your *pièce de résistance*."

Trella had been working on the gown in secret, not even showing it to her mother or Gili. It was understated, like her makeup, with a high waist to cover her bump and a simple bodice with cap sleeves. The seed pearls and crystals had been the time-consuming work and she was proud of how it had turned out.

Her hair was in a loose chignon. Her mother placed a bridal comb over her ear in lieu of a veil. The brushed silver flowers with pearls and diamonds was a family heirloom, not ostentatious, just right for a small afternoon wedding.

They followed the ever-efficient Mario to the palace chapel.

Xavier was already there, speaking to the bishop. He wore a bone colored tunic-style jacket with dark gold epaulettes and gold leaf embroidery at the cuffs and hem. His royal red sash sat across it, decorated with a number of pins, including a key and a family shield. A sword hung off his hip.

*My prince*, she thought, and ached inside.

He wasn't, and he never would be.

*  *  *

Xavier turned and splendor kicked him in the stomach.

Her dress was white, which somehow wasn't ironic despite being a maternity gown. Perhaps it was the fact her bump was still modest, or the way the gown drew his eye to the beading at her neckline and across her shoulders. The detailing resembled angel wings but also projected strength. Delicate armor.

The rest of her was incandescent. Her skin held the warm glow he had noticed the night they'd met, as if firelight reflected off a creamy nude. She was both waif and warrior. Goddess and maid. Infinitely fascinating.

She came forward, expression guarded as she introduced her mother.

Elisa Sauveterre was a tall, elegant woman of Spanish ancestry with sensual features and a single streak of white in her black hair.

As she held his hand in both her warm ones, shadows in the misty depths of her eyes told him she had feared this day would never come for her daughter. It made him feel churlish for bristling when Trella had informed him her mother was coming.

"It's an honor to have you here." He was embarrassed now that his grandmother wasn't attending, and that they hadn't extended an invitation for Elisa to stay at the palace. His impatience with himself sharpened his tone as he told Trella, "You look beautiful."

Her mouth tightened. "Thank you." But she might have been speaking to Mario who handed her a bouquet.

Mario was Xavier's witness, which suddenly felt like a disregard for the significance of the occasion. Xavier understood ceremony. His entire country was up in arms, wanting to witness this moment. The least he could have done was invite a friend to be his best man. He might not have many friends, but he had some.

Friends would come next year, though, when he married Patrizia in a spectacle he already dreaded.

Today's occasion was far more to his liking, even though the exchange of words seemed to hold extra power when spoken in such an intimate setting, heard only by the three witnesses. Even those few extra pairs of eyes and ears fell away as he spoke directly to Trella, losing himself in the shift of gray and green in her irises.

When she said, "I do," it reverberated within him, so visceral he knew that he would feel bound by this promise his entire life. She was his responsibility now, but he would have to turn away from her to perform the rest of his obligations. The war of dueling duties already hammered a crack into his psyche, causing a schism that would never heal.

"Do you have the ring?" the bishop asked.

"I'll only have to remove it when I go into the hospital." Trella waved off the case.

It was an unexpected swipe of claws at a part of him Xavier hadn't realized he'd exposed. What did he care that she didn't even glance at the ring he'd spent more than an hour dithering over, wanting it to match her sparkling, multi-faceted personality?

Her mother's tiny sniff broke the silence. Mario smoothly withdrew the ring. The bishop quickly finished the ceremony.

"You may k-kiss the bride…" Everyone had got the memo this was not a conventional marriage.

Her wary gaze grew even more vulnerable.

Should he have forgone this custom? Probably. But he set his hand at her waist and drew her toward him.

She braced her forearm along his and clenched her fist into his jacket sleeve, leaning on him for balance as she offered her mouth.

He brought his hand to the side of her neck, felt the cool tickle of a few strands of hair, and reminded himself not to make a fool of himself. Keep it brief.

He nearly groaned at the onslaught of sensation when his mouth covered hers.

As tenuous as everything else might be, in this second, they were as united as they'd been in Paris. Everything in him wanted to deepen and ravish, requiring all his willpower to keep the kiss short and sweet.

Her mouth moved under his with equal restraint, but he tasted the desire for more in the way her lips clung to his. Paradise hovered like a promise, but he couldn't surrender to whatever this thing was between them. All he could have was this. One kiss.

And it was already over.

"Mario tells me you wish to cancel Australia." The Queen looked up from her breakfast. "Why?"

He *had* cancelled, if Mario had done his job. Xavier filled his plate and gave the butler a nod, sending him from the room so they could speak in private.

"Don't play dumb," he said as the door closed. "It's an important initiative."

Unlike some of his counterparts, the royals of Elazar took specific, active roles in government. His entire year had been a series of trade talks in various regions. It wasn't appearance for the sake of it, but business meetings and presentations to push for expansion of existing agreements that would keep his country from going bankrupt.

"She isn't due for weeks," his grandmother continued. "Even when she goes into labor, what help do you think you will be?"

"She's alone in a strange country, stuck in the hospital. I'm not leaving for a month of press interviews where the first question will be, 'Why aren't you with your wife?'"

"Is that why you visit her every day? Because I'm told she keeps herself amused. Drawing. Chatting to family. You wouldn't be missed."

Perhaps not. Even Trella had asked if he was only visiting for appearances' sake.

The press release on their marriage and impending parenthood had been short and vague, playing to concern for a successful pregnancy without going into detail. It had made Xavier sick to hear his team discuss how spinning the pregnancy as a miracle would create a groundswell of support, overcoming judgments about a scandalous, ill-timed affair.

Trella hadn't reacted beyond a remote, "I've played this game a long time. Say whatever you have to."

She had played the isolation game as well and did know how to amuse herself. He wasn't needed and didn't know why he counted down the minutes until he could dodge the paparazzi on the hospital steps and enter the guarded sanctum of her room.

Her prison was as cozy as it could be made. Monitors and equipment feeds were tucked behind panels. The walls were a comfortable mocha, the blankets printed with Elazar's national pasqueflower—the white buttercup that grew wild in their alpine meadows. Trella even wore regular clothes rather than a functional hospital gown.

But she reclined on the bed twenty-four-seven. Rising to use the toilet or shower was all the activity she was allowed.

Because of potential rupture.

Her doctor had scared the hell out of him when Trella had been admitted, explaining the need for such vigilance.

Trella had been stoic. She had checked into Hospital del Re the night they'd married and, despite only having resided in his apartment for a week, he'd felt her absence. Why? She'd been angry with him, cool when she'd been forced to speak to him, but somehow she had infused a sense of liveliness to the palace. The sound of her laugh in another room, or even just the splash of color from an abandoned scarf, made it less of a museum and more of a… Hell, it had always been his *home*. How could it suddenly feel like one?

He shook off the impression.

"You're very well-informed," he said, realizing the silence was stretching. "Yet you've never once asked *me* how she is."

"How is she?" She used her among-the-people tone of fabricated warmth, smile inching toward supercilious.

*Anxious*, he wanted to say. Trella *was* keeping herself busy, but he read the stress that lingered in the corners of her mouth and the tension between her brows.

"As well as could be expected."

"Then you should be able to leave her."

"I know what you're thinking." He shook his head. "I'm acting like a decent human being, not becoming attached."

Yet he was indulging himself with the visits. She hadn't asked him to come.

*I've done this before*, she'd said of her seclusion, then had revealed her best coping strategy. She was an accomplished sketch artist.

*Practice*, she had dismissed when he went through her book. He'd been taken with each image. Some were graceful gowns, some intricate patterns for beadwork. Some were colored as brightly as a children's book and others were shades of gray.

Then he had found one of their wedding day, copied from a photo her mother had taken. Trella's hint of a smile as she gazed up at him held shy awe. He wouldn't call his expression tender, but there was no hiding that he was absorbed by her doe-eyed stare. The captured moment was uncomfortably revealing, yet honest enough he couldn't be ashamed.

"I meant that for Mama, but I think you should hide it in the palace, to be discovered a hundred years from now. Give the art historians something to get excited about." She tore the page from the book and signed it. Her conspiratorial grin as she rolled it had tugged at him to play along.

It had been the first time she'd warmed up to him since their marriage, eyes sparkling with the vivacity that had first ensnared him in Paris.

He'd accepted the drawing with the strangest tingle of pleasure, liking the idea of her being resurrected generations from now, pulled from the footnotes and celebrated.

For a moment, there'd been nothing between them but this frivolous secret they were planning to keep. Then, as their gazes stayed locked, sexual awareness had crept in. The attraction was still there, ignored and subverted, but in those seconds, he felt the lava churning below the surface, swirling and burning, building with pressure against the cracks.

"Surely you can make arrangements with one

of her family members if the round-the-clock care at the hospital isn't sufficient?"

He snapped back to the breakfast room and his grandmother's facetious tone. The heat in him faded.

"I've discussed that with her." He had suspected Trella was homesick after catching her tearily viewing photos of her infant nieces. "Her brother and his wife are tied up with their new twins. Her mother is on hand to help them. Her sister can't leave her new husband." They were trying to get pregnant, if Xavier was reading the subtext correctly. "And something has gone off the rails with the brother who was engaged. She'd rather not speak to him, so…"

"You're being manipulated."

"By whom?" He held her gaze, turning one of her best weapons—barely disguised derision— against her.

"You have obligations," she began in a very quiet voice that held no hint of a tremble. It was the very lack of emotion, the stamp of inarguable logic, that made her words so powerful.

The splinter he had experienced on his wedding day rent deeper, ringing with agony as he felt himself stretched on the rack of conflicting duties. Wife. Crown. Temporary commitment. Eternal service.

A sharp rap on the door had them turning

their attention to Mario as he stepped in without waiting for an invitation.

"Apologies, Your Majesty, but the Prince is requested to go the hospital. Immediately."

"They're prepping her for surgery," he was told when he called from the back of his car. He broke into a sweat and urged his driver to hurry.

He was shown to a lower floor when he arrived. She was in pre-op, flat on her back in a hospital gown, hair covered in a blue cap, lips white, tubes taped to her arm.

"You made it." She held out her free hand.

He grasped her fingers, disturbed to find her grip clammy and weak. "What happened?"

"Pain. Tearing. They scanned and said it has to be now." Her mouth trembled.

Thirty-four weeks. So early.

"Shh." He leaned to shelter her, trying to smooth her tense brow with his thumb, but feeling the trembles coursing through her. "Are you having an attack?"

"No," she choked. "This is real fear, Xavier."

"It will be okay," he insisted, undone because she had every right to be scared and there wasn't a damned thing he could do. *He* was scared. "I'll come in with you."

*What help do you think you will be?*

"You can't. I asked."

How did that reach inside him and squeeze his lungs dry? Her wanting him with her spun and wrapped and pierced his heart like a barbed hook, deeply uncomfortable, but inexorable, tethering them together. "I'll come in anyway."

"You *can't*, but listen. I asked them to wait until you were here so I could ask… I've texted my family. Tell them how it goes as soon as you can. If I don't make it—"

"Of course you'll make it." He closed his ears against any other outcome.

"*Listen*. If I don't, swear to me you'll give the baby fair time with them. They'll need it." Her eyes filled. "Our baby deserves to know what love is."

Her words punched a hole clear through him, leaving an expanse of emptiness that was replaced with agony. The gentle rebuke in her eyes was another blow, searing and brutal, too painful to withstand, too impactful to avoid.

"You're going to come through this," he managed. What if she didn't? He couldn't even.

"Promise me on everything you hold sacred. Your crown. Everything." Her nails dug into the back of his hand.

"If you need to hear it, yes. I'll take the baby to your family myself." He would promise anything to ease that terror in her eyes. To ease his own sense of failure. Of being so lacking she had no faith in him to give their child what it needed. Their baby *did* deserve to know what love was. If she wasn't here to offer it…

"Sir, we have to take her now."

"Kiss me goodbye," Trella whispered.

He swooped without hesitation, felt the tremble in her pouted lips, thought he ought to be gentle, but he took. Ravaged. He invaded her mouth with his tongue and drowned in all she was, trying to slake a hunger he feared would last all of eternity. Her lips opened, surrendering, even as she responded, flavoring the kiss with sweetness amid the shared desperation.

He kissed her as though it was the last one they would ever share. He couldn't bear the thought that it might be.

"Sir—"

He straightened abruptly, feeling the loss like he was torn away by a tornado, hating that he was forever doing what *must* be done.

Trella covered her mouth with her wired hand, eyes blinking above her white fingers. She kept her grip on his fingers until she was forced to let go.

"Sir, there's an observation room for students. Let me show you."

A nurse showed him to a small room with a window. Beyond, he saw Trella nod at the anesthesiologist before her face was covered with a mask. Her doctor motioned gloved hands to the team then everyone moved into place so all he saw were backs clad in scrubs.

"It shouldn't take long," the nurse said. "If you feel lightheaded, there's a chair."

He ignored her, all his attention on the surgery.

"They're waiting for confirmation she's out," the nurse said. "There they go."

They began to move in a controlled, efficient way and the nurse was right. In a very short time, the doctor was handing a tiny, naked infant to the nurse standing by with a towel. The nurse angled the baby to the window, showing him it was a boy.

The anguish in the small face at being separated from his mother pierced Xavier unexpectedly. He felt ridiculously helpless, wishing he could comfort the boy.

"We've been preparing for a premature birth. He's small, but that attempt to cry is a good sign. That's the pediatrician who's taking him. He'll run tests and place the Prince in an incubator then come speak to you. You'll probably be able to hold him. Your son, I mean," she said with a wry attempt at humor. "Not the pediatrician."

*Son.* Xavier nodded and texted Trella's family, including his grandmother.

A boy.

It seemed such an inadequate few letters for the magnitude of what was happening to him. He had a child. A son.

His phone buzzed with returned texts from Trella's siblings, congratulating him and asking after her.

He glanced up and something had changed. The team around Trella had snapped into frantic action. The anesthesiologist was clearly alarmed and the surgeon's movements became agitated. Through the glass, he heard raised voices issue sharp commands.

"What happened?" Xavier slapped his hand to the window, even as his gaze looked for the door to enter the room.

"Sir, I—" The nurse made as if to close the curtain.

"Find out what's happening."

"Of course." She hurried away.

He pressed his forehead to the cold glass, terror snaking to squeeze his heart. He strangled on the one word he managed to whisper.

*"Bella."*

## CHAPTER EIGHT

TRELLA CAME TO in a blurred awareness of voices and stark white. Even Xavier looked carved from pale marble, his blue eyes translucent as antique glass. Bottle blue, she wanted to call it. She should use that shade in next season's collection.

Why was he leaning over her like that? So close and grim?

"Baby?" She tried to say, but there was no sound. Her voice had evaporated.

"Fine. Really well, considering how small he is." He backed off as a nurse picked up her wrist, but his eyes stayed locked on her.

*He.* "A boy?" That came out in a raspy whisper.

"Yes."

She blinked heavy eyelids and tried to smile. "Sadiq."

"What?"

"He saved me." She was becoming aware that she was stoned. Recreational drugs weren't her thing, but she'd been prescribed so many pharmaceuticals to quell her panic attacks that she knew what this foggy haze was. She hated it and fought to think through it. "I wouldn't be here without him."

"Dr. Lagundo saved you," he snapped.

"Why are you mad?" She frowned, startled to find the nurse was still beside her, fussing with her arm. Whatever she did hurt, but distantly. "Can I see him?"

"Soon." The nurse seemed familiar. Her smile was nice, but Trella couldn't recall her name.

She hated drugs. Hated being dopey and disassociated. She ought to be upset as Xavier's remark belatedly penetrated. "I almost died?"

"There were some tense moments," the nurse said. "Your doctor will tell you more. I'll let her know you're awake."

She left and Xavier came back to her side, mouth pinched.

"Are you angry that I pulled through?"

"What? No! Why would you think that?"

She tried to think through a brain made of cotton balls. "You don't like me. You're mad about the baby."

"None of that is true." He loomed over her again, very intimidating. If she wasn't so spaced-out, she would think he sounded tortured. "You scared the hell out of me."

Was he holding her hand? Something cupped

her fingers in warmth. It was nice. She liked the gentle stroke across the back of her hand.

"But it would have been easier for you." She was briefly thankful for the drugs because despair didn't overtake her. "I make things harder. I don't mean to. My family forgives me because… I don't know. They love me, I guess. But you don't, so it's okay if you wish I had died."

"Stop saying that. What would Tyrol do without you?"

"Who's Tyrol?"

"Our son."

She frowned. "I expected a girl."

"I texted you the name a couple days ago." He sounded disgruntled. Maybe self-conscious. "You said you liked it."

"When? I hate drugs. They make me so stupid. Is it Tuesday or Wednesday?"

"Wednesday. I texted on Monday and asked what you thought of Tyrol or Trentino." He seemed to be petting her arm, combing his fingers into the gaps between hers. "They're family names. You said you liked Tyrol. We're *not* naming him Sadiq."

"But picture your grandmother's face if we did."

He choked out a laugh, turning his face away, shoulders shaking. "You're funny when you're high, I'll say that much."

"You should laugh more."

He looked back at her with an expression she couldn't decipher. Regret maybe, but something like appreciation?

She closed her eyes against his sorcery.

"Did you know, *bella*? Is that why you said those things before you went in?"

"I don't get into trouble on purpose," she grumbled, ignoring the number of times Ramon had accused her of doing exactly that. "And I don't apologize when I do. It makes people feel good when they help me. My whole medical team is feeling super heroic right now."

He let out another incredulous laugh. "That is some seriously backward logic. Exactly how ripped are you?"

"Admit it. This morning you were ambivalent about having a son. Now you're grateful. You're welcome for the clarity."

Stunned comprehension seemed to blank his face, but she didn't gloat.

"I want to see him." She weakly squeezed the hand that gripped hers. "Is he beautiful? Does he look like you?"

"He looks mad." His voice wasn't quite steady. More emotion shifted across his profile, things she couldn't interpret. Concern? "He wants you."

*It's the drugs*, she warned herself, even as her heart turned over with sweetness that he might feel something on their son's behalf. *Don't start seeing things that aren't there.*

She didn't doubt he'd been worried on some level when he thought she would *die*. He wasn't a monster, but he had made it abundantly clear that his heart was beyond reach. He was capable of kindness, but that was the limit.

His phone buzzed. "That's your family. I'll let them know you're awake. Smile." He held up his phone to take her photo.

She stuck out her tongue and crossed her eyes. "Tell them we named him Sadiq."

"That's the friend whose wedding you attended earlier this year, isn't it? His wife would object, wouldn't she?" He tapped the screen.

"She would stab me in the eye. That's why it's funny."

"I'll tell them his name is Tyrol." He leaned down to press a kiss between her brows. "I like your eyes the way they are."

"Xavier?" She touched the side of his head, keeping him from straightening. "It's really confusing when you're nice to me."

His thumb traced near the corner of her mouth. "I never said I didn't like you, *bella*. You do make things hard. All of this is hard. But I am grateful for our son."

*And me?*

His eyes were an endless blue that only grew

more intense the further she fell into them, but even in her muddy-minded state, she knew better than to ask.

And he didn't say.

# CHAPTER NINE

XAVIER LEFT FOR Australia ten days later.

Trella and Tyrol were released from the hospital and went directly to her family's compound in southern Spain. Her brother was in
residence with his four-month-old twin girls.
Her mother was there, along with a team of
nannies and servants and guards. Xavier could
not have arranged better, safer care for either
of them.

Trella had bounced back from near-death with
startling cheer, pouring such tenderness and joy
over their son Xavier almost thought it was fake;
it was so far removed from anything he had ever
experienced himself. Her words from pre-op
kept echoing in his head. *Our child needs to
know what love is.*

Did he? Because the limited feelings Xavier
had allowed himself to feel toward her had am-
plified his fear when her surgery had gone sideways. This level of concern for someone wasn't

comfortable. Was he a bad parent for setting up his son to love and possibly to lose?

*He* needed distance as a buffer against becoming more deeply invested in both of them so he went to Australia as scheduled. He hated every single one of the thirty days he was gone, which only underscored why the separation was necessary, he supposed.

It didn't help that things went exactly as he had warned his grandmother they would. He answered the same question so many times he muddled his lines at one point.

"The plan was tripped last year."

The blond newscaster tittered.

"The trip was planned," he corrected, yanking his mind back from Spain to Adelaide and the trade talks he'd been in. "The early birth made it possible for me to travel as scheduled. I was on the brink of canceling, which would have been a shame."

Several handshake deals were already moving toward more formal agreements. His adherence to duty was producing much-needed results.

"But you must miss him!"

"Technology is a wonderful thing. We check in often. He's thriving and Trella is recovering. That's the most important thing." He flicked a glance at one of his handlers, silently conveying that if they didn't swerve back to topic, this interview was over.

The newscaster took the hint. "We wish them well. About your meeting with the state representative today…"

Did he miss his son, Xavier wondered later? If such an emotion had never been acknowledged, internally or externally, did it register with anyone if it somehow manifested today?

How *could* he miss the boy? Tyrol was an infant who wanted to suckle and sleep. Trella was adept at keeping Xavier apprised of their son's progress, such as it was. She texted often, telling him about a gain of an ounce or other small milestones. She sent him photos—probably half a dozen a day. A more pragmatic man would say one was plenty, but Xavier found himself studying each one, fascinated by tiny eyelashes and miniature fingernails. The boy's eyes looked like his own, but his mouth was definitely Trella's.

One grim night, Xavier let himself recall that for a few moments, this boy's resemblance to his mother had been all that might have been left of her. The despondency that had engulfed him at the thought had had him placing a video call to her.

She had been surprised since she usually initiated the calls if she happened to be nursing and the time was right on his end. She had asked him about his day, which he didn't care to talk about, and he had listened to whatever she volunteered, silently mocking himself for being riveted by small talk about her family and a few shower gifts.

There shouldn't have been any holes of curiosity or unmet sense of obligation within him. His wife and child were well. He was getting on with his life exactly as he should.

So why did he nearly go through the roof when he woke to a fresh message from her?

Ramon and Izzy are getting married! The wedding is at the end of the month, in Madrid. We decamp to the family mansion the day before I'm due to return to Elazar. I'll extend our stay until after the ceremony since it's only an extra weekend.

On the surface, it was a perfectly reasonable assumption. Moving her and Tyrol with the rest of the staff to Elazar for a few days so she could turn around and go back was a needless expense. Royal detractors would have a field day. She was nursing, so she couldn't leave Tyrol in Elazar while she attended the wedding. Xavier had no reasonable basis to refuse her request.

Nevertheless, the only word that came to mind was, *No.* He didn't analyze it, he only knew he would not go back to the palace and wait for her.

* * *

As the youngest, Trella sometimes thought she
had received all the leftover DNA after her siblings had taken the best of it. Henri had their
father's sense and logic. He was stubborn, yes,
but *she* was outright obstinate. Ramon had their
mother's passion and determination, but Trella
was an opinionated hothead. Gili scooped up
all the sensitivity and generosity while Trella
selfishly stole all the attention with her nervous
breakdowns.

None of them were small-minded or jealous,
but Trella—the baby who was spoiled and de-
ferred to all the time—was drowning in envy
of all of them.

Why couldn't she have a partner in parenting
like Henri had with Cinnia? Why couldn't she
have a big wedding that had everyone buzzing
with excitement, like Ramon was planning with
Isidora? Why couldn't she have a husband who
not only couldn't keep his hands off her, like
Kasim with Gili, but refused to have any other
woman by his side as he took the throne of his
country?

Why did she have so much negative self-talk
eating away at her self-esteem? *They* didn't.
They were all better and smarter than that.

She was the broken one.

With her arms braced on the side of the pool,

she gave desultory kicks behind her while watching Cinnia hand off a freshly fed Rosalina to Henri.

"I'll put her down and work through siesta. You'll finish your lunch then rest before we travel?"

"I will," Cinnia promised, smirking at Henri's overprotectiveness before he erased it with a tender kiss. "Thank you, darling." She gave her wrap dress a final straighten and turned back to the salad she'd been picking at while nursing.

Henri glanced at Tyrol, asleep in the cot in the shade. "Do you want me to take him up? You should sleep before we leave, too."

The flight was an hour and Trella was five weeks postpartum, but her scare during delivery had set them all back to watching her like she was made of spun glass.

"I'll take him when Cinnia goes up. The weather won't be as warm in Elazar. I want to enjoy the pool while I can."

"I'm going to miss you when you go back to Elazar," Cinnia said as Henri left.

"I know. This has been really nice."

Quite by accident, Cinnia had been the first to know Trella was pregnant, when she had been hiding her own pregnancy from Henri. They had become very close in those early months and sharing these weeks of new motherhood had deepened their sister-like bond.

"Is it going to be okay living there, do you think?" The simple question was the reason Trella loved Cinnia. Her sister-in-law invited confidence but didn't intrude.

Trella sighed, daunted enough by the future to admit, "I have no idea. I feel good. Physically, I mean. And stable, mentally. But I'm *here*. That always helps."

"At least I knew Henri when I was in your shoes." Cinnia had been Henri's mistress for years before her pregnancy tore them apart and drew them back together. "It must be hard, having a baby and still being at the getting-to-know-you stage. You two haven't had a proper chance, have you?"

"No." Two nights and daily hospital visits that she'd said she didn't need.

She had, though. She'd soaked up his duty visits like sunshine, trying not to read into the kiss they'd shared when they wed. He'd seemed to be pretending it hadn't happened, sticking to chatting very generally about whatever meeting he'd been in or whatever political scandal was trending.

When he'd gone through her sketchbook, she'd felt very vulnerable, especially when he found the one she'd done of them. Why had she thought it was a good idea to give it to him? He'd probably thrown it out, but she had longed so badly for him to feel *something* about their wedding day.

He'd looked…touched? Whatever the softening in his face had been, it had caused her to moon so obviously, he'd flinched and looked away.

She was such an idiot. He was probably feeling put-upon. When they did connect over the tablet, he had seemed remote. He wasn't impatient, but she had the sense his prevailing mood was resignation.

She was trying to resign herself as well. Years of therapy had taught her to focus on one small piece of the future at a time. When he had crushed her soul with his news that their marriage would be temporary, she hadn't tried to imagine what her life would look like after their divorce. She had focused on making it to term with her pregnancy.

Once Tyrol had arrived, she'd come here, where she'd been able to focus on Tyrol and her recovery. Returning to Elazar and her looming divorce wasn't something she was ready to contemplate. She didn't even know how to handle the two and a half months left in their brief marriage!

Making a concerted effort to include Xavier in Tyrol's progress had seemed like the right thing to do. She told herself it was her way of encouraging a bond between father and son, but she knew there was a part of her that liked having an excuse to reach out to him. She was still trying to push for something that was futile.

But just when his reticence had her convinced he felt nothing, he would surprise her by phoning to ask how things were going. He would linger on a video call after she'd run out of things to say, seeming content to stare at a sleeping baby over a screen.

Such a confounding man.

She glanced to where Tyrol slept; the one thing in all of this that made her unspeakably proud. If everything she'd been through in her life, all the pain and traumas and anguish had had to happen in order to bring her son into this world, so be it. She accepted all of it.

"Has your doctor really forbidden you to have another?"

"We talked it over several times through the pregnancy. It was my idea that she would tie my tubes during delivery, so I wouldn't need another surgery in the future. She did. I'm not sorry, or even very sad. I resigned myself a long time ago to not being able to get pregnant. He's truly a miracle. The delivery was such a near miss, though. I wouldn't want to push my luck, especially now he's here and needs me."

Cinnia nodded. "What about a surrogate? I'm sorry. Maybe that's not something you'd consider?"

"Gili told me years ago she would be my surrogate, but that was before Kasim." She tucked her chin. "Can you imagine his reaction?"

"He gives her anything she asks for." Cinnia closed her grin on her fork. "His head would literally explode trying to decide whether to be possessive or indulgent."

"Right?" They both chuckled, then Trella sobered. "They would want to secure his heirs before even thinking of it, anyway. I don't see Xavier wanting to wait." *There is a reason for a spare.* "Maybe I'll find a surrogate someday, but I don't think that would change Xavier's mind about us. It's not just about another baby. We're not you and Henri." Or Gili and Kasim. Or Ramon and Isidora. "He has other considerations."

*He doesn't want me.*

She *had* to accept that.

It made her chest grow tight, though. Her throat ached. She ducked under the water to hide how she was tearing up. She stayed there, diving deep and crawling along the bottom until her lungs were about to burst, only coming to the surface when she reached the stairs.

"Pah!" She stood and wiped the water from her eyes.

Cinnia had come to her feet and was saying hello to someone.

Henri had returned with a striking blond man in tailored dark gray pants and a collared T-shirt that hugged the fit muscles of his shoulders and revealed his tanned gorgeous biceps.

The newcomer glared at her from his familiar, laser blue eyes. "Should you be *swimming*?"

Suddenly dizzy, Trella panted, "*Hola, cariño. I missed you, too.*"

Xavier was distantly aware of Henri retreating with his wife, but if the woman had a name, he had already forgotten it. His entire focus was eaten up by the way Trella rose from the water like Venus herself.

Water sluiced down her body, washing away the grinding aggravation that had propelled him here. He had needed to see her without understanding why. He might have labeled it homesickness if that wasn't such a juvenile emotion and he was in Elazar, not a part of Spain he'd never seen before.

But he'd come here with single-minded determination and when he'd finally clapped eyes on her, she'd been on the *bottom of the pool*, trying to give him a heart attack all over again.

All his concern, pining and every other thought

in his head drained away, however, as she walked toward him.

Coming here was a mistake. He saw that as clearly as he saw she wore a red bikini, the triangles of fabric tied off at her hips and between her breasts. She had been quite comely with the weight of a baby distending her middle, always turning herself out stylishly, even when she'd been in the hospital.

Keeping his mind off sex while she'd been in a delicate condition had been, if not easy, at least quickly forestalled by worst-case scenarios. He had told himself any attraction he still felt was a byproduct of his not having had sex since they'd made the baby sleeping in the cot to his left. Maybe the two kisses they'd shared had ambushed his memory when it was least convenient. Definitely, he relived their night in Paris far too often.

It all added up to an obsession he should have put behind him by now.

He hadn't.

Her approach coiled him tight. He hadn't seen her naked since Paris and her hourglass figure was as spectacular as his libido recalled. Better. Glittering droplets sparkled on her golden skin and her breasts were positively voluptuous, swaying as she padded toward him, bare feet slapping the tile.

His mouth watered. A distinctly male pulse tugged behind the fly of his pants. He had to resist a telltale swallow and consciously regulated his breathing. The animal, that restless beast that had been scratching and digging inside him, howled as she drew near, wanting to leap on her. Reunite.

"What are you—?" She was squeezing water from her hair, but as she met his gaze, her eyes widened in reaction, pupils exploding like fireworks. Her breath caught, expanding her chest and drawing his attention to her nipples, already sharp from the chill, but poking even harder under his gaze.

"Wh-what are you doing here?" Her hand went to a nearby chair back as if she needed to steady herself.

He was acting directly against his responsibilities, despite the rationalizations he'd concocted. Angry with himself for the hunger clawing through him, he searched his brain for the reasons that underpinned his arrival.

"I'm taking you to Madrid. You'll stay with me there."

Her shoulders fell. "You don't trust me?"

That wasn't it, but he didn't want to admit—even to himself—that he hadn't been able to wait three more nights to see them. Not just his son. Her.

He found his gaze straying to the curve of her hips and the dip of her navel and forced his attention to drag across to the infant in a pale green onesie. The strangest yank in his chest had him stooping to pick up the boy.

The sleeping baby gave a small start of surprise, fingers splaying, then relaxed into a warm ball against the hollow of Xavier's shoulder. He felt heavier. Sturdier.

"He's growing."

"He is." She wrapped a towel around her middle, hands shaking. "Xavier, I swear I wasn't trying to avoid coming back. The wedding is a rushed thing. Izzy's father has been ill. It's a big deal for him to be able to walk her down the aisle so they're indulging him. It's also the only chance for the bunch of us to be together for the foreseeable future. That's why I need to be there."

"I'm not saying you shouldn't go. But it's your first public appearance since we married. We should be seen together."

"Well, of course you were invited. I just didn't think…" She was taken aback, which was justified, he supposed. "Doesn't it send the wrong message?"

Because of the way their press release had been worded.

*Given Ms Sauveterre's preference for avoiding the spotlight, the marriage is a formality to ensure the legitimacy of Prince Xavier's heir and won't be continued in the new year.*

"I've spent a month having my devotion to my family questioned. I'd like to change the optics." There. That was the excuse he had given his grandmother and he stood by it. Their countrymen were going mad over the three photos he'd released of the young prince, but they were questioning why he wasn't spending more time with him.

Trella understood how the PR game was played. She wouldn't fault this move.

The warmth that had pinkened her cheeks drained away, though. Her expression stiffened. "Of course. And we both know how unimpeachable your sense of obligation is. Most of my packing is done. I only have to shower and change. Shall I send a nanny to take him? After you've had time to post some selfies, of course."

He had set himself up for that, but it still landed on target. "I'll keep him," he said in a tone that let her know she was walking a fine line.

She flipped her wet hair and walked away.

Trella fell asleep on the flight so they were in Madrid before she was alone with Xavier again.

Physically she was recovered, but Tyrol was so little he needed to feed often, even if that meant waking him. She was up several times a night so tended to nod off midday. But rather than dozing, she would have preferred to spend the time working through Xavier's surprise appearance.

Optics? Really? It was incredibly insulting. Her entire family had been used a million times over to sell magazines and promote products, all without their consent. She was tempted to tell him what she thought of him, but part of her disbelieved him.

For a minute, as they'd stood by the pool, she'd thought—But, no. His carnal look had been gone once he'd picked up Tyrol. She had imagined it. What kind of wanton did it make her that she had responded to blatant lust, anyway?

She *had* responded, though. She had run to the shower to cool off, slowing the race of her pulse and willing away the thrumming awareness in her loins.

Fat lot of good it did. Flutters of intrigue were still playing like butterflies in her middle, gaze straying to the cut of his pants over his butt and the sculpted muscles beneath his shirt as he paced in front of her. She had missed him!

Tyrol finished nursing and was fast asleep so she unlatched him and handed him off to a nanny, then she struggled to put herself together behind the screen of a receiving blanket that didn't want to stay in place.

Yes, I'm half-naked under here. *Stop staring.*

A flush of heat went through her. It was a lusty reaction that had simmered at merely sensual while she'd been feeling squat, scared and vulnerable in a hospital. Or when he'd been on the other side of the planet.

Now she was more confident on so many levels, but still unsure of herself with her husband. This was as bad as his ambush in Innsbruck when he'd left her with nowhere to hide.

"Ready?" he said, tucking away the phone he'd been tapping while she'd nursed.

"For?"

"I've been waiting to look around. I haven't seen the house, either."

"Oh. Um, sure." The mansion was on a small estate in La Moraleja, farther out of the city from the historical home in the Salamanca neighborhood that had been in her mother's family for generations. This house was built with old-world touches like columns and wrought iron rails, but it was very modern, perhaps only a few years old.

"Did you lease it? Or…?" Surely he hadn't purchased something for a long weekend?

"It belongs to a friend. We studied architecture together. He showed me the plans a few years ago. I'm interested to see how it all came together."

He waved for her to lead him from the lounge to a small dining area that was likely used for intimate lunches. The gallery that overlooked the main door was above them. A row of tall windows afforded a view of the landscaped grounds.

"I didn't know you were interested in architecture." She watched him take in the elevator, set in a convenient location, but made unobtrusive by disguising it with the rise of the stairs. Why did a bit of small talk make her so nervous?

"I'm an architect."

"Really! What have you designed?"

"My chalet." He bypassed the entrance to the kitchen and opened a door to the patio, inviting her to exit ahead of him.

"You did well. I liked it." A wind had come up beneath the overcast skies, making her hug her arms and try to tuck her wayward hair behind her ears as they walked past flower pots that lined the covered pool.

He was looking sideways at her.

"I wasn't trying to escape because I didn't like the floor plan."

He rolled his eyes, which made her smile, but self-consciousness stuck like a burr, prickly and sharp. It was strange to be with him again, in person, alone, without nurses or valets hovering. With sexual awareness sizzling within her.

"I'm serious," she said, trying to hide her nervousness. "I know you don't need my approval, but I thought it felt cozy despite the open plan. You obviously placed the windows very carefully. Each view was a well-framed photograph of the natural world—what?" she demanded as his look grew penetrating. "I'm an artist. I notice when care has been taken for a particular effect. Don't you? Look at these stairs."

She waved at the way they curved down from the upper terrace.

"Most people see convenience, but the placement balances the turret on the other side, which is probably the master bedroom, situated to overlook—" She turned to look across the expanse of grounds, charmed as she noticed the brook and the wooden bridge. "Oh, that's lovely, isn't it?"

"He wanted to put the master bedroom on this end," Xavier said. "At the top of the stairs, closer to the pool. I suggested the turret and told him to curve the stairs."

She pivoted to face him, watching his gaze track the upper terrace, profile dark with critique, but also…envy?

"What else have you designed?"

"Nothing. My attention is needed elsewhere." He said it without emotion, but she felt the pang that he refused to betray.

"You're frustrated."

His lids came down so the heat of his gaze glowed fiercely behind the veil of his spiky lashes. "We're talking about that, are we?" His attention dropped to her mouth.

Suddenly they were poolside again. Such a hard streak of sexual heat shot through her, it physically stung from the base of her throat, behind her breastbone, sank like a hot coal in the pit of her belly and radiated warmth into the juncture of her thighs. Her heart took off at a gallop while birds took flight in her midsection.

"I meant as an artist!" She blushed, embarrassed at how quickly and blatantly she reacted to a simple look.

His mouth deepened at the corners. He pushed his hands into his pockets. "There are many ways to apply form and function to the role I occupy. I don't have to design something."

"It's not the same." She was still flustered, stewing in heat and being confused by it. "I told you about the time I was depressed? It was because the medication made it impossible for me to create. The need was there, but when I sat down to draw or sew, it was like sending a bucket into an empty well. I wasn't having panic attacks, but I didn't see any point in being alive if I couldn't…" She held up her hands.

"I'm not depressed."

"But you're denied."

"So what?"

"It's something you need."

"It's something I *want*. Desire can be ignored in favor of more important things."

"We're not talking about architecture, are we?" She let her hands fall and blinked, eyes watery from the wind. Or so she hoped he believed.

A long silence followed where only a distant wind chime rang.

"Are you really here because of optics?" It made her lungs feel heavy and raw.

He hissed out a long breath. "I came because I wanted to." He set his teeth after he said it, as though absorbing some inner thought that displeased him, then said in a voice rife with subdued turmoil, "But we don't get everything we want, *bella*. You know that as well as I do."

He wasn't mocking her. He was saying it with deep understanding of the things she would never have—a carefree childhood, another pregnancy. She choked up, wanting to ask if he had come because he'd wanted to be with her, but she was too scared of the answer.

So she only said, "Have you forgotten my name? You're calling me *bella*."

"It's not an endearment. It's who you are. It's what you are." The last bit sounded as though it came out against his will.

She wanted to believe him, but her misshapen heart was so very conscious of her flaws. Of the fact he had rebuffed her.

"I've never felt beautiful." She toed a pebble. "I was the messy one, always grass-stained and needing my hair combed. After my kidnapping, the press called me 'the fat one,' because I comfort-ate. I starved myself in retaliation and cut my own hair and looked like a Goth for years, dark circles under my eyes, makeup smudged and face pale from not sleeping properly. It took ages after I got my panic attacks under control to look as healthy and happy as my sister."

She squinted as she looked up, startled to find she had his full attention. That wasn't pity in his expression, though. He was engrossed, which made a squiggling sensation tremble in the pit of her stomach.

"You asked me that night in Paris, remember? You asked if I was as beautiful as my sister. I thought it was funny to say yes because I was impersonating her. The only time I feel beautiful is when I look like her." She knew better intellectually, but deep down, she still had a lot of demons.

"You were stunning when you were pregnant.

You're beautiful now. When I saw your sister in Berlin, I thought she was beautiful because she looked like you."

She shook her head. "You didn't even know—"

"I *knew*. I could tell the second I saw her. I just didn't believe it. I thought—"

"What?" She held her breath, brimming with dread and hope, not sure what she wanted to hear.

He grimaced. "I thought I'd been a fool. That the way we'd reacted to each other had been a one-off thing."

She swallowed. "It wasn't?"

His gaze slammed into hers, pupils expanding the way a cat's dilated before it pounced. Lines of tension pulled the rest of his face into the harsh countenance of a barely restrained barbarian. "Clearly."

She stood on a tipping point, vibrating under the strain, drawn, drawn, drawn. The pull in her chest was nearly irresistible. A prickling wash of sensations made her hyper aware of everything around her, the pale heat of the sun, the scent of the grass, the dampness in the air and, most especially, the way he was looking at her mouth. At the way such a tiny expression of interest from this man could send wildfire through her whole body.

She tore her gaze from his, seeing only a blur of green and blue.

"Please be careful, Xavier." She scraped at the hair tickling her cheek, shaken. "My self-esteem is full of holes. Don't give me hope if there is none."

"For what? You don't want to be married to me. You said so."

"I don't want to be married to a man who doesn't want me." She had to press her lips tight so they wouldn't tremble. Meeting his gaze was hard. She couldn't hide the struggle, the longing, that was eating her up. "If you do…"

"I don't *want* to want you," he ground out.

She jerked back as though he'd struck her. He winced.

"I mean I can't *afford* to want you. My father followed where sexual interest led. It was a disaster. I didn't expect this," he grated. "I wouldn't have come."

She breathed through each of the blows, eventually able to ask, "That's all you feel?" The question was too revealing. She regretted it, even before he answered.

He took a long time, then, "Don't hope, *bella*. You know my views on love."

His gentle reply broke her chest open, leaving her heart pulsing like an open wound. *This* was what she had been avoiding accepting. This was why she couldn't bear to look into her future. He was never going to love her.

Engulfed in agony right to the backs of her teeth, she nodded dumbly. "Will you listen for Tyrol when you go in? I want to see the bridge."

She didn't notice the hand he reached out as she walked away.

# CHAPTER TEN

HE HAD HURT HER. He hadn't wanted to. Cruel to be kind, he had thought, and he had regretted it immediately. What could he do, though? Admit that what he felt was not purely sexual. Even if he was capable of love, which he wasn't, they had no future. He couldn't lead her on.

He hated that he'd returned her to that stiff wariness, though. The woman who had texted without hesitation for the weeks they'd been apart suddenly had a full schedule and little to say. By the time they were at a dinner hosted by the bride's parents the next evening, the tension between them was palpable. Her family smiled around it.

Angelique hadn't arrived yet, Henri was there with his wife and twins along with her mother, and Trella spent most of the evening needling Ramon.

Xavier tried to intervene at one point. Ramon wasn't above getting personal in retaliation and neither was Trella. It was escalating, but the bride, Isidora, tugged him aside. She was a stunning woman with auburn hair and a smile that put anyone at ease.

"It's a rookie move to get involved. Better to ignore them. Trust me."

He waited until they had left to ask Trella, "Why were you being so contentious with Ramon?"

"I wasn't. That's how we communicate." The passing streetlights flicked over her stoic expression.

"I thought you might bring on an attack."

"No." She sounded petulant. "We fight like that all the time. It's fine."

"It wasn't because you're angry with me?"

Silence, then, "I'm not angry. I'm hurt."

He should have left it there, but said, "Either way, you should take it out on me, not him." *Punish me.* He couldn't stand the guilt he was carrying.

"I'd rather fight with Ramon." Her hands twisted in her lap. "I know he won't let me win. Any points I score, I've earned. It builds my confidence. And no matter what I say, he'll still love me. I don't have that kind of trust with you."

*Be careful what you wish for,* Xavier thought, flayed to the bone. He didn't speak of it again.

\* \* \*

Trella was a dam filled to the brim, gates stuck. When Xavier bowed out of joining Ramon and his racing friends at a sports bar the next evening, the pressure inside her climbed a notch higher.

"The bar isn't Kasim's thing, either. I invited him to come over with Gili for the evening after they see Mama. Cinnia wants to give the girls a quiet night so she's staying in." Trella desperately needed time with her sister. "Do you mind?"

"You're not going clubbing with the bridal party? I'll stay with Tyrol."

"Isidora will have enough paparazzi as it is. If Gili and I went? We're doing her a favor staying away."

"I see. Of course. Invite them. That's fine." They were being exceedingly agreeable and polite since she'd admitted to her hurt feelings last night. It was horrible. She kept wondering how she would endure two more months of this. A lifetime, really. Would it be worse or better when they divorced and lived apart?

She was so caught up in her own turmoil, she completely forgot that Xavier had met Gili before. *Gili* hadn't, the darling. She rushed him when she arrived, taking both his hands to say beseechingly, "I'm so glad we have this chance to clear the air. I can't imagine what you thought of me in Berlin. You must have been so shocked. But I hope we can be friends because I already adore your son."

Her sister's warmth could melt glaciers and Xavier's expression eased in a blink. "It's already forgotten," he assured with his patented charm.

Trella felt a stab of jealousy. Why couldn't she win him over as easily?

Gili turned to her then, concern in her eyes, because of course she had picked up on Trella's distress. At the same time, something glowed from her like a beacon, a happiness so bright, it blinded.

*Oh, Gili.* Anytime Trella thought she couldn't survive whatever anguish was gripping her, her twin found a way to lift her out of it. Smiling tearily, she hugged her pregnant sister tight.

Xavier was glad to have an evening with the King of Zhamair. Asking Kasim about a complex situation in one of his neighboring countries was a welcome distraction from his struggle between duty and desire. Between wanting to mend fences with Trella and letting her bruised feelings keep her at a distance.

Thirty minutes in, he realized the women hadn't come back from fetching Tyrol. "Did we bore them? I'll find—"

"Please let them be," Kasim said. "She needs time with her sister."

"Which one?" Xavier asked dryly, hoping Trella wasn't shedding tears over him.

"A fair question." Kasim took up his drink. "Their interdependence takes getting used to, doesn't it? But this…" He chucked his chin toward the ceiling, where the women were likely in Trella's room. "She was bursting at the seams."

"Pregnant?" A surprise rush went through Xavier. He was astonished to realize he was pleased for the couple. Why? It had nothing to do with him.

Except that he knew how good it felt to have a child. It struck him then how important Tyrol had become to him. Not because he secured Elazar's future, but because Tyrol was… Tyrol. Not an insurance policy for the future, a relation.

Disconcerted, he had to clear sudden emotion from his throat as he rose to shake Kasim's hand. "Congratulations."

"Thank you." Kasim darkened with a flush of pride and hitched his pants to sit again. "It's very early days, only confirmed the day before we left Zhamair. Not something we're making public."

Xavier fetched his own drink and offered to tap glasses, experiencing envy as he thought of Kasim sharing the moment of discovery and every single day of the pregnancy, along with the birth. Feeling robbed was not a new sensation for him. He got over it quickly, but he wondered if Kasim realized how lucky he was, able to go through this process as many times as his wife was up for.

He could, too, he supposed, with Patrizia.

His brandy tasted like snake venom. He abandoned it.

"I'd like you to consider something," Kasim said, sounding like someone unused to requesting favors. "Closer to the birth, I'd like Trella to come to Zhamair."

A strange void opened in Xavier. "We won't be married any longer." It took enormous effort to state that with equanimity. "Trella may go where she pleases." The knowledge knotted his gut.

Kasim's smile tightened. "I expect she'll want to bring Tyrol. I know Angelique will want to see him by then."

Which would require Xavier's permission. He instantly rejected the idea. He had sent Trella to Spain while he'd traveled Australia before he'd realized how unbearable it would be. The King of Zhamair was not plotting to steal his son, he was sure, but at least if Tyrol stayed in Elazar, he knew Trella would come back.

He looked away, disturbed by the dependence that train of thought suggested.

"It was very hard on Angelique to be apart from Trella when Tyrol was born." Kasim took a healthy sip of brandy, like he needed it, and hissed out his breath. "She fainted when Trella flatlined. Then your text came through and I realized why. She was hysterical until Trella was revived."

*So was I*, Xavier could have said, but they were already sharing far past his usual level. He loathed thinking about those long terrifying minutes. It put him in a cold sweat.

"I'll see what I can do," he said woodenly, mostly to end the discussion. Doing a favor for one of the most powerful men in the Middle East was a smart move, he reasoned, but was repelled by the idea of using his son for political gain.

*Duty*. It wasn't a double-edged sword. It was two branding irons pressing him front and back, pinning him in place, allowing no escape and only sinking deeper into his flesh when he tried.

Much later, when the couple had left, he was still thinking about where the line was drawn. Would his grandmother say Tyrol was doing *his* duty by going to Zhamair, cultivating warm relations with a foreign entity?

The poor boy didn't even know what he was in for. He lay unswaddled in Trella's lap, gaze wandering the ceiling, arms flailing and fingers catching in the curtains of her loose hair as she looked over him.

"Who gets another cousin?" she asked the boy with soft excitement.

Xavier sat with his feet propped on the ottoman. Her top afforded him a lovely view down her cleavage and her gentle laughter was as erotic as her tickling hair might feel, sweeping across his skin. It was sheer torture to sit here, wanting without having, but far too soon he wouldn't even have this much so he savored the pain.

"Did you know she was pregnant? Before she told you? Kasim made it sound like you have a supernatural link." He was skeptical, but Angelique had called her that time in the car, seeming to know Trella's panic attack was upon her.

"Was he worried I spied on them while they were making that baby?" She lifted her head, so stunning, with amusement curving her lips, that his heart lurched. "No, it's nothing like that. More an emotional thing." Her smile faded. "I should have realized how happy she was, but I've been distracted."

Pensive because of him. Upset. At least she was talking to him again.

"Do you feel it with your brothers?"

"They're too pigheaded, especially Ramon. Isn't he?" she said to Tyrol. "*Tio* Ramon is a *toro*." A bull.

"But you still love them." Xavier was beginning to see how love wasn't just a romantic notion, or even a desire, for her. It was as vital to her as oxygen. It drove the very blood in her veins.

"I love them very much," she agreed, sober and ultra-gentle as she kissed Tyrol's bare feet. "They got me through my darkest times. I hung on because of them. Pushed through *for* them. Now I have Tyrol." She dipped to nuzzle his tummy, making his little arms jerk.

*You have me*, Xavier thought, but thorns had invaded his windpipe. He was starkly aware he couldn't pledge anything more than the pittance he'd already offered.

"You never wished for brothers or sisters?" Her head came up. "Your mother didn't have more children?"

"My father has a daughter. Maybe three or four years old by now? My mother has two boys. Teenagers, I think."

"You've never met them?"

"There's no place for them in my life." That's what he'd always thought, but he heard how cold it sounded, especially as she looked so askance.

"You could have made one."

"What would I have in common with them?"

"*Parents*?"

"They didn't act like parents." He shook the cubes of ice in his glass, wondering if he could judge when he'd barely grasped the ropes himself. "Neither were a great example of the importance of sibling relationships, either. I was young, but I picked up on jealousy and resentment between my mother and her sister. Because of her marriage into royalty, I suppose. And my father lost his brother."

"It wasn't his fault, was it?" She gathered Tyrol to her shoulder, tucking his blanket around him. "How old was he?"

"He was sixteen, his brother was eighteen. It was just a bad wind that came up while he was sailing. My father didn't talk about him often, but when he did..." Xavier swallowed, still affected by the memory of his father growing teary. "He missed him. Made me think I was better off without that kind of risk."

"But you'll give Tyrol a sibling."

"I have to." It was the stark truth, but again he heard how indifferent it made him sound when really his emotions on the matter were so tangled he couldn't even begin to name them.

Her brows pulled together and her mouth pouted. "I'll do it because I *want* to."

Without his need for biological children, many options were open to her, adoption among them. He suppressed a flinch, surprised how much it hurt to think of her starting a family with another man.

"You should," he made himself say. "You're

a natural at motherhood. Family is clearly your source of strength."

She stared at him like he was a dog that had been hit on the highway.

"Are you going up?" he asked, trying to change the subject. "Leave him with me. I'll put him down when he falls asleep."

Her mouth twitched, but if she was surprised at his desire to hold his son, it was quickly blinked away. He let out a breath as she placed the boy's warm weight in his hands, relaxing as he embraced one of the few responsibilities he was pleased to have.

Trella hovered, watching Tyrol rub his fist against his cheek, chasing it with his mouth. They shared a chuckle at his efforts, but Xavier's was bittersweet.

"My family was not yours, *bella*. The way you are with them is a foreign culture to me. I can't emulate something I never had. But I do want Tyrol to be happy. Happier than I was."

Her hand settled on his shoulder. It was unnerving not only because they hadn't touched since she'd been in the hospital, but because she gathered the torment rippling through him into a hot ball in the corner of his chest, so it pulsed under the feathery weight of her fingers. He held very still, as if her hand was a shy bird and he didn't want to startle her into flitting away.

"I know." Her thumb moved in a brief caress. "And I know you're starting to love him. I'm glad."

His heart swerved as her hand lifted and he watched her retreat.

Trella was trying hard to resign herself to Xavier's limitations. Gili had hugged her and wiped her tears and said, "Give it time." Things had been rough between her and Kasim before they'd married. *She* wasn't ready to give up on Trella finding happiness with Xavier, but that was Gili. She wanted to believe the best of everyone and everything.

Trella wasn't so sure, but she took heart from the way Tyrol had begun prying himself through Xavier's defenses. Xavier took every opportunity to hold his son. Not for optics. No one was seeing him walk down the hall in the middle of the night. He *wanted* to hold him. He expressed concern about a little spit-up, then worried the damp patch would make Tyrol uncomfortable and changed him. He talked to his son about architecture, for heaven's sake, then broke off when he realized Trella was listening.

Still, when she had accused him of starting to love his son, she suspected he had been more surprised by his capacity to do so than she was.

And therein lay the problem. She had told him

she didn't want to be married to a man who didn't want her. She had meant a man who didn't *love* her. If there was a chance he might develop feelings for her, surely she owed it to Tyrol to give their marriage a chance?

Or was that a foolish rationalization because she was smitten?

Either way, she had to keep the struggle off her face and smile for the wedding photos. Ramon and Isidora's marriage should be perfect, even if hers wasn't.

The ceremony was held in a five-hundred-year-old cathedral, conducted by an archbishop, witnessed by royalty, aristocrats, heads of state and celebrities from film, stage and the athletic arena. The route to the hotel, where the reception was held, had been blocked off and was lined ten-people deep with bystanders, photographers and even television cameras. Drones buzzed between the cars and a helicopter pattered overhead.

They hurried from the cavalcade up the red carpet, past the deafening cheer of the throng behind the velvet ropes, through the security checkpoint and into the relative peace of the ballroom where they finally caught their breath.

Mirrored tabletops reflected the lush floral arrangements of orchids and roses. Wisteria dripped from the ceiling along with crystals that glinted like snowflakes. A harpist's delicate notes welcomed them along with uniformed staff carrying trays of gold-rimmed glasses of champagne.

"That was insane," Xavier said, not dropping his protective hold across her back.

"Small wonder I've never been on a date before, isn't it? We're a nightmare to take anywhere."

Surprise loosened his clean-shaven jaw. "You never dated? *At all*?"

"Well, there was this one stranger I met in Paris." She gave him a cheeky wink and made a tiny adjustment to his boutonniere. It was a delicate creation of spotted feather and red-throated orchid with a lacy fern frond behind it. She deliberately avoided looking at the red sash that scored his chest, announcing his station—the role that was more important than she could ever hope to be.

"Seriously? I'm the only one?"

She shrugged. "One of Ramon's friends recovered from a crash at Sus Brazos two years ago. I ate dinner with him by the pool a few times. We kissed once, but it was…"

"What?" His fingers dug into her hip, something flashing in his eyes as his expression grew unreadable. She wouldn't let herself believe it was possessiveness.

"Nothing. Over before it started. Like you and me." Affair, pregnancy, marriage. They were all slipping like sand through her fingers, refusing to be slowed. "But thank you for coming with me tonight. I should have said that before. I was dreading coming alone and having to dodge awkward questions about our marriage."

She made herself smile and meet his eyes as she started to step out of his embrace. His arm hardened.

"The things I'm still learning about you," he muttered. The fingers of his free hand looped around her wrist. He looked across the room, expression tight then came back, fierce and hot. "I hate this, *bella*. We had one damned night that was perfect. The only regret I had was that I didn't have more time to get to know you better and now we have time and we're wasting it."

Edginess came off him in waves, rattling whatever defenses she still managed to hold up against him. Her bottom lip grew wobbly and she had to tuck it between her teeth. "I thought you were just putting the time in, waiting for us to be over."

"No." He shook his head, voice deepening. "No, I'm… I'm trying to protect you."

"Oh, Xavier." She sighed. "I'm *tired* of being protected. That's why I slept with you. I wanted to feel what other people feel. The ones who aren't sitting in a vault waiting for their lives to start. I wanted to flirt. Feel pretty. Dance."

"Go on a date?"

"Yes."

His thumb stroked the thin skin inside her wrist. "This is a date."

*Not a real one*, she thought. People who went on dates were hopeful of a future. But beggars couldn't be choosers. She forced herself to make a face of forbearance as she said, "It's not dinner and a movie, but I suppose it will do."

His expression relaxed, lips twitching. "Too cliché. I've brought you star gazing." He deliberately let his attention scan the growing crowd of celebrities.

Relief as much as amusement sent laughter bursting out of her. She slid her arm around him, hugging herself into him as lightness filled her. "If you promise to have me home by curfew, then yes, I would love to be your date."

*Over before we started.*

These last few days had given Xavier an unprecedented glimpse into Trella's world. She was right. All too soon they would be strangers again. He couldn't countenance it. Like his last night of freedom in Paris, he was compelled to grasp this chance with her.

Unlike Paris, he couldn't steal her away and it was delicious torture standing beside her, setting a subtly possessive touch upon her, but unable to do more. All the while, he fell under her spell, as did everyone she spoke to.

It was humbling, in a good way, to be with a woman whose attention was as valuable as his own. Rather than having to consciously include her in a conversation, they operated as a unit. One minute she introduced him to a family friend with a pedigree that matched his own, the next he was catching up with a diplomat he'd dealt with in the past whose wife was a client at Maison des Jumeaux.

Then they were interrupted and she threw herself into a man's arms. "Sadiq!"

The man's wife, who happened to be Kasim's sister, Xavier learned, was clearly a close friend, too. They spoke with the couple for a long time, until Xavier couldn't wait to dance with Trella again.

"Explain to me exactly how he saved you?" He prompted when they were on the floor.

"Hacking." She glanced around as she said it. "We're not supposed to talk about it. He still does some high-level work on the side. He found out where I was being held and alerted the police."

"How old was he?"

"Fifteen. Crazy to think of, isn't it? He didn't know us very well, either, just had some classes with the boys. I think it was the challenge of it. He's stubborn that way. It definitely wasn't a desire to be a hero because you can see how self-effacing he is. But he wanted to help and persevered until he had something. Every time I see him, I'm reminded that he gave me this life and I should be grateful for it. Not waste it."

She met his eyes as she echoed what he had said earlier, but he read the deeper question in the longing look she gave him. They'd been engaging in subtle foreplay all night, not pawing each other, but neither shy about taking the other's hand or pressing close. He'd watched her nipples harden and heard her breath catch and felt the goosebumps that rose on her arms under the brush of his hand.

God knew he was aroused just by her nearness, never mind the scent that had hardwired itself into him or the way watching her quick mouth as she talked and laughed made him want to kiss the hell out of her.

He touched her chin then couldn't resist letting the backs of his fingers slide down the heat of her soft throat. As he let two fingertips rest on her pulse, the one that confirmed she was alive when she might very well have been lost and he never would have known her at all, he wondered how the hell he was ever going to say no to her again.

## CHAPTER ELEVEN

TRELLA CHECKED ON Tyrol as soon as they arrived at the mansion. He was sleeping soundly, completely oblivious to the potential shift in his parents' relationship.

As she stood over him, she thought of all the reasons her marriage was impossible. Progeny, publicity, even Xavier's rejection of love over duty. His refusal to open himself *to* love.

She thought of all the ways she was broken, but miracles happened. This tiny boy, for instance. She owed it to him to try with his father, didn't she? Really try to reach his heart?

Was it a rationalization? Perhaps. She couldn't deny that lust was alive and well inside her, but so was something deeper and more nascent. She didn't want to believe it was love. Not yet. Not when she was about to risk rejection. Not when there was every chance she would have to spend her life yearning for a man who might very well be incapable of the emotion.

"How is he?" Xavier asked in a whisper, coming up behind her.

His need to see his son fed her hope that he was more than capable of deeper feelings.

"Perfect," she answered, watching his profile soften as he looked at Tyrol.

"He is," he agreed, turning up the flame of desire inside her.

She led him from the room, heart hammering, and went to his room, not her own.

*"Bella,"* he protested as he followed, but stayed in the open door, backlit by the light from over the stairs.

"Close the door, please."

He sucked in a long breath, like he needed it to face a Herculean task. "I can't. You know I can't."

"I don't want to make a fool of myself in front of the guard in the hall."

He pushed the door shut and leaned on it, breath hissing out. He was a dark shadow in the unlit room. She saw his fist close against the hardwood next to his thigh.

"Can you even make love?"

"As of midnight, yes," she said ruefully.

His head thumped back against the door. He swore. "You know this is impossible. You know——"

"I do." She went to him and picked up that

rock hard fist, gently rubbing his fingers, trying to coax the tension from his hand. "But who else am I going to have sex with? Hmm? Who else do I trust with myself?"

"I still don't understand why you ever did."

She kissed his fingers. "Because no one else makes me feel like this." She set his open hand above her breast, where her heart raced. "If it's not the same for you—"

"It is, damn you." He hooked his hand behind her neck and dragged her closer, voice growing hoarse. "No one else has *ever*—"

He covered her mouth with his, cutting off whatever he'd been about to say.

She didn't care. All she cared about was being up against his lean, powerful body, feeling him devour her mouth as though it was the only thing he would ever need. It was an onslaught, his hand shifting to her hair to drag her head back. His other arm crushed her into him while his lips ravaged and his tongue invaded.

Her heart knocked into her rib cage, sending sweet pulse beats through her arteries, weakening her limbs. She felt helpless, but not to him. To this yearning. Lethargy stole her strength when she longed to cling to him. All she could manage was to crush the edges of his jacket in her fists and moan into his mouth.

He made a jagged noise and dragged his teeth

along her generous lower lip, tugging then releasing. "I'm being too rough."

"I need to know you feel the same. I want you so *bad*. You have no idea."

"I do." Another rough noise scraped from his throat. He dragged up the skirt of her gown, so when he picked her up as he pushed off the door, her legs were free to twine around his waist.

"But it's only lust, *bella*. Tell me you understand that."

She was on the verge of laughing, loving his easy strength. Her self-assurance slipped a notch, but she could feel him hard and straining between her legs. It was too beguiling to ignore, making her tighten her arms and legs, trying to increase the pressure there. "Whatever it is, I need it."

He walked her unerringly to the bed and came down to settle his weight on her, mouth sealing to hers again. Writhing under him, she tried to touch all of him with her whole body, tried to drag his clothes out of the way while searching for hot naked skin.

"Slow down." He grabbed her hands and pinned them over her head, then dragged his mouth along her jaw, down her throat and bared her breast for his fierce gaze. "This will *not* end before it starts." He used his teeth on the swell of her breast, making her shudder. "I've fantasized about it too many times to rush now that I have you where I want you."

A surge of moisture hit her loins. "I think about us when I'm in the bath."

He lifted his head and with a hiss said, "You witch." He levered up and rolled her over, swept her hair out of the way then slowly tugged open the ties behind her neck. "Tell me exactly what you do when you're in the bath." He set kisses down her spine. "Be specific."

"I could show you." She lifted into his hardness.

He grasped her hip and met her pressure with thrusts of his own, breaths thick and animalistic as he ground his erection into her soft cheeks. Then he slid a hand under her bunched skirt and across her stomach, fingers delving beneath her silk panties as he settled on her again. "Keep moving," he said, gently sawing two fingertips between her damp lips, mouth planting wet kisses on her nape. "Show me how much you want me."

She did. She rocked herself between his hand and his heavy hips until she was trembling with desire. She stopped, shaking with arousal. "I'm so close. I want to feel you inside me."

"Not yet." He shifted and settled his hand deeper, so his fingers slid inside her, so satisfying yet maddening. "Keep going."

Helpless to her own body, she did, until she was releasing broken cries, fists clenching the blankets, body clasping uncontrollably at his penetration, shivering and completely lost. Utterly his.

"So good," he said, licking between her shoulder blades, still mimicking lovemaking with light thrusts of his hips, drawing out her orgasm as he kept his hand in place. "I want you in a thousand ways. There will never be enough time for how much I want you."

And he called it *only lust*?

She pushed against the mattress, trying to twist beneath him. He withdrew his hand, but hooked his fingers in her panties and pulled them down and off, sitting up on the edge of the bed to throw them away, then he shrugged off his jacket and kicked off his shoes.

She knelt behind him and reached to work down the buttons of his shirt. He turned his head to catch at her mouth with his, easily distracting her. Their tongues met and the heat kept growing, not appeased in the least. She sobbed and he turned to scrape his hands down her shoulders, brushing her gown away so she knelt in a puddle of near-black velvet.

He stood then, chest expanding in deliberate breaths between the edges of his open shirt, as if he strained to keep control of himself. "Don't ever ask me again if you're beautiful. Know it, *bella*. You are the kind of beautiful that could topple a kingdom."

He reached out and wound her hair around his hand then bent to kiss her.

She tried to balance the bitter with sweetness in her own kiss, but her desire was too potent. It was all lust. He pulled back to yank his pants open then stripped, checking for a moment with one hand and reaching toward the night table.

"I can't get pregnant," she reminded.

He snorted and found a condom anyway, tearing it open with his teeth.

It shouldn't have made her want to cry, but it did.

*"Bella,"* he chided as he pressed her flat and used a knee to part her legs, "I'm protecting *you*."

It didn't feel like it. But when he stroked his tip against her, hot and beguiling, he seemed to send electric lines of pleasure radiating through her. She forgot to be outraged or hurt. She set her hands on either side of his head and kissed him. Extravagantly. Invitingly.

And when he sank into her, it was her turn to bite his lip and groan.

"I'm going to make it last," he said into her mouth. "All night."

"Yes, please…"

* * *

Mario met them as they entered the palace. He smiled benignly at Tyrol, who was fussy after the travel, and said to Xavier, "The Queen expects you. She'd like to hear about Australia."

Completely attuned to her husband after their night of lovemaking, Trella felt his surreptitious sigh.

"Of course." He glanced at Trella from eyes bruised by their sleepless night. "Eat. Get some rest."

She nodded and followed his retreat with her gaze, feeling as though he took her heart and spun it out like twine behind him.

All of her felt undone and achy. They'd had one conversation in the dawn light, bodies still damp with exertion, while her nerve endings had still been singing with joy.

"You know this doesn't change what has to happen." His voice had been grave, his body steely against hers.

She had shifted her head on his shoulder. "I know. But I'm not sorry. Are you?"

"I'm trying to be."

She had turned her lips in to his throat and they had started all over again.

"Gerta can take the Prince up to the nursery, Ms. Sauveterre," Mario said as they arrived on the second floor.

*Signora Deunoro,* Trella longed to say, but it had been agreed from the outset that she would not change her name. After Tyrol's christening, she was to receive an honorific title of *Dama*, the lowest of Elazar's ranks. A future monarch could not have a parent who was common.

"I'll keep him. He's having an off day." And she was feeling neglectful after leaving him in Gerta's care during the wedding last night. "You go settle in," she said, since Gerta hadn't actually seen where she would be living in the palace. "I'll bring him when he's ready for a long nap."

With a curtsy, Gerta followed Mario's direction to the nursery level while Trella turned toward the room she'd occupied before she'd gone into the hospital, the ones adjoined to Xavier's.

Mario cleared his throat. "You're in the dowager's wing now, Ms. Sauveterre."

*This doesn't change what has to happen.*

Speechless, composure fraying, she let Mario escort her across the gallery, through a pair of doors, down a long hall where paintings of Xavier's ancestors watched her progress in silent judgment, and through another set of doors.

The temperature grew cooler as they walked. Tyrol's fussy cries echoed off the high ceiling with the sounds of their footsteps. She didn't try to soothe him, just let him express exactly what she was feeling, and was viciously pleased to see Mario's obsequious expression grow more and more strained.

She understood that the dowager's wing had been deliberately placed to provide as much distance as possible between former queens and new ones. It wasn't a horrible place. It had been prepared for her occupancy with cheerful floral arrangements, a new sofa and her very own lady's maid, Adona, who was eager to prepare her some soup.

Mario offered a quick tour, pointing to a bright, empty room as a potential studio, if she wanted to provide a list of items she would like placed there.

"A crib and a change table," Trella said, growing as fractious as her son. "Tyrol needs a nursery."

Mario tilted his head in a way that was unbearably condescending. "Royalty inhabits the royal wing."

"I see." She sat on the sofa and dug in her shoulder bag for the receiving blanket she carried. She shook it out with a snap then tucked a corner into her collar as she met Mario's gaze with a challenging one of her own. "And do I go on safari to the nursery to feed him? Or does he exercise his lungs through the palace every two hours as he is brought to me?"

Tyrol was showing off the growing strength of his lungs, recognizing the feeling of the soft flannel against his cheek as she draped it over him and growing frantic for her to open her buttons.

"It was understood the Prince was taking a bottle," Mario said, mouth pinched, gaze averting self-consciously while his whole face went red.

Oh, was he uncomfortable with her breastfeeding? What a shame.

"He'll *need* a bottle, won't he? Or he'll starve to death before we get to each other. Am I even allowed into the palace without an escort? He's *six weeks old*. Still a few days shy of his due date. He's not weaned and won't be for a *year*."

"As I see." Mario cleared his throat and turned to the door. "I'll leave you to it."

"Do."

*This doesn't change what has to happen.* Xavier should have told her *this* was going to happen. How *dare* he use her up last night, thinking this would be okay.

Trella woke thick-headed from a heavy nap to hear Xavier's hushed voice, "Give him a bottle if he needs it." A door closed.

She jackknifed to sit up and shot a look to the travel cot she'd had Gerta bring down from the nursery. It was empty.

Sucking in enough breath for a scream, she leapt from the bed and stumbled into the lounge, wearing only the oversized T-shirt she'd thrown on for sleep. Xavier was there, but no one else. No Gerta, no Adona, no *Tyrol*.

"Oh, *hell* no," she informed and rushed after her son.

"Trella." He caught her arm and reaction kicked in. She used the momentum to round on him, heel of her hand aimed straight for his nose.

He deflected, tried to catch her into a hold, but she expertly twirled out and broke his grip, the movements ingrained in her muscles from years of practice. Knocking a lamp in his direction to force him to leap back, she backed up too, out of his reach, neatly balancing on the balls of her feet, breathing in hisses as she gauged the distance between him and the door and how she would take him out in order to get there.

"I didn't *know*," he growled, holding himself in ready stance. "*Calm down*."

"Bring him back." She reached for a slender vase and flicked its three tall irises at his feet, spattering water on the bottoms of his pant legs, then tested the heft of the blown glass as a weapon.

"You're going back to the room you were in, next to mine. I sent him up because he needs a bath. I stayed to tell you that and keep you from throwing a righteous fit when you woke and saw he was gone. Calm the hell down."

"You should have told me last night this could happen. This, by the way, is how you put up a fight." She shook the vase at him, mocking his lame attempt to turn her away last night.

"This was always going to happen!" He pointed at the door. "If not today, soon enough. In a few weeks, you'll move out of the palace and he'll come and go between us. That is reality, Trella. I have damned well made that clear to you. More than once. *You* came to *my* room, last night, knowing that. Don't pretend this is news."

She threw the vase at the fireplace so it shattered and droplets of water made the dancing flames sputter and crackle. Then she stared at the destruction, chest heaving.

"Is this bringing on an attack?"

"Don't pretend you care if it does."

"I *care*," he bit out. "Why the hell do you think I'm here?" He looked positively tortured as the words escaped him. He wiped his expression away with a stroke of his hand, releasing a heavy sigh.

"I've just been raked over the coals for *one* photo." He held up his finger. "And because a debate has sprung up online. Team Trella or Team Patrizia. My fault." He turned his hand to tattoo his chest with his finger. "I promised to undo all of that, as if it's even possible, and walked back to my room to learn you'd been sent here. Do you know how much furniture *I* wanted to break? Do you understand what I'm doing, taking you back there? It's pure weakness!"

No, it wasn't. That's not what caring was. He wasn't ready to hear or believe it, though, and she was too angry and hurt to explain it.

"Why does she hate me so much? Why—?"

He closed his eyes. "I keep trying to tell you. Emotion has nothing to do with it. It can't. That's the point."

"The crown is all that matters."

"Yes."

"I hate your crown! I hate that our son will be raised with this same hard-hearted attitude."

"Hate away. It changes nothing."

"And you want me to come to your rooms again, anyway."

"Yes."

"Even though it won't change anything, either."

"Yes."

Mouth trembling, she knew that, like him, she didn't have a choice. She would go with him and believe what she believed, that he would change, and one of them was going to lose.

She nodded jerkily, but before she could step forward, he leapt to meet her, not letting her walk through broken glass to get to him. Then he was cupping her cheek, tilting her lips up to the hungry weight of his own. She moaned, knowing what that taste was now. That narcotic that filled her with hope when he kissed her. *Love.* She was madly, deeply, hopelessly in love with him.

# CHAPTER TWELVE

"You're neglecting your duties. The Australian agreements have completely fallen apart." His grandmother had called him on the carpet before he'd even digested his breakfast.

"Both parliaments have risen for the year. The committees adjourned," he said.

"Yet I am informed the deadline is the end of the year. If it's not finalized, we start over in the new year." She held out a missive.

He took it and quickly gathered how certain opportunistic corporations were manipulating the fine print, trying to push Elazar into a stress position and a renegotiation that would be advantageous to their own interests. She was right. He should have caught on when the meetings had begun experiencing delays two weeks ago.

"This is the first I'm hearing of this," he muttered.

"Because you've been distracted. Dating. *Shopping.*"

He gritted his teeth. Trella was preparing to move her design house's head office to Lirona. The fashion industry was waiting with baited breath for her to purchase her property. Real estate and tourism would boom the minute the new fashion district was born. Squiring her to potential locations, ensuring the choice worked as well for Elazar as it did for her, fell right into Xavier's trade negotiation bailiwick.

His grandmother ought to be thanking Trella, but she only said, "Mario has set up an emergency meeting of the council. You're expected at ten o'clock. We cannot afford to lose this, Xavier."

*Duty.* It was killing him. Quite literally chipping away at his flesh. His belt had had to go in an extra notch and the scale had him four pounds under his usual weight. He had no appetite. Of course, he was on his wife like a stallion with a mare every chance he got. No wonder he was skin and bones.

Bristling with culpability, he returned to his apartment. He would have to hurry to make the meeting, but he was more aware of the clock ticking down on his marriage.

In a few days it would be Christmas, his one and only with his son's mother. Then their marriage would melt away like snow under rain. Gone, gone, gone.

He nodded at Vincente to leave his jacket on

the bed and dismissed him, then he went through to Trella's room, where he slept every night with her naked body resting against his. They tried to keep a low profile but were fooling no one, except possibly themselves. Despite the intensity and excruciating pleasure and profound satisfaction they gave each other, they had to keep rising and moving apart.

Soon that would be permanent.

*Not yet.* His hand closed in a tense fist. He wasn't ready.

"I have to run to a meeting—" he began as he entered.

She sniffed and turned with surprise. She had showered while he'd been to see the Queen and wore only a slip. She was on the phone.

"*Esta bien, Mama. Te amo,*" she finished and signed off, then swiped her cheek.

His heart lurched. "What's wrong?"

"Nothing." She turned away for a tissue. "Ramon and Isidora arrived safely at Sus Brazos. Gili and Kasim will be there tomorrow."

And this was her first year apart from them. She was homesick. She didn't have to say it. He watched her wither daily, saying nothing because they both left many things unsaid, aware their days with each other were numbered. They didn't want to waste them with animosity and problems they couldn't solve.

Guilt assailed him, though. He was *stealing* time with her. Neglecting his duties while he neglected her needs. He pinched the bridge of his nose. "If you want to spend Christmas with them, you should."

"With Tyrol?" She brightened.

*"Bella."* He hated saying no to her, but it echoed in his voice. "You're upset. You miss them." She was going to need them more than ever soon.

"I can't leave him! He's still feeding in the night. I would miss *him*." She waved in the direction of the nursery, where a nanny took him for a bath every morning while they ate breakfast and started their day. She softened her tone, her expression so vulnerable she put an ache in his chest. "You could come."

*You're neglecting your duties.*

"No, I can't." This was it, he realized. The fracture that had begun working its way through him on their wedding day began to cleave open, tearing him apart. *But he had no choice.* "The Deunoros spend Christmas here."

"And I'm not a Deunoro. Why should he spend Christmas with her? She hasn't even looked at him since—"

"Leave it."

She buttoned her lip, but the glare she sent dropped the room temperature lower than it had been on the sleeting day of Tyrol's christening.

He couldn't let her bring it up because he was ashamed of his grandmother's behavior. Rather than the traditional pomp of open-topped carriages and a public stroll with the future monarch back to the palace, they'd all traveled by car. His grandmother had come in her own, arriving last and leaving first. Exactly one photo had been taken of Queen Julia standing with her grandson at her side and her great-grandson in his bassinet. Trella had been left out of the picture.

He closed his eyes, afraid he couldn't do this if he looked at her. His voice was hoarse with strain. "You should go see your family and come back to the new house."

He heard her breath suck in, sharp and mortal. "No, Xavier. Not yet."

"I was hoping we could get through Christmas, but we're only putting off the inevitable."

"What about…" Her voice faded. "What about a surrogate?" He had seen her afraid before, but not like this, with her throat exposed while she offered a knife.

He had to consciously remember to breathe. "It's not about another baby, *bella*."

His own composure threatened to crumble as her chin crinkled and her eyes filled. She caught her mouth into a line to hide its tremble, then that glorious Valkyrie in her came forward, steeling her spine and refusing to be cowed.

"I'm not leaving Tyrol. I'll move into your stupid ugly house if you make me, but I'm taking him with me."

That stung more than it should. He hadn't been able to design a home from greenfield for her, which felt like a breach of duty in itself, but he'd personally overseen all the renovations and security upgrades to the one he'd bought. He'd taken the utmost care with every detail.

"Don't make this ugly. The agreement is three and a half days each." That was not renegotiable.

"You're *busy*. Why should someone else feed him a bottle when he could be with me?" Oh, she was fierce when she wanted to be. Flushed, with her eyes glimmering, she threw the forces of nature at him. "At least I *love* him."

"So do I!" It exploded out of him. Within him. *Nothing* would come between him and his son.

She threw her head back, fury fading into sorrow. "But you don't love me. I can live somewhere else."

He jerked his head to the side, slapped by the torment in her voice.

"Say it," she choked. "Tell me these last weeks of…" She waved at the bed where they had writhed with passion. "I have tried *so hard* to show you we could make this work. Every breath I take is carefully measured to make sure I don't impinge on your role in any way. I should bite my tongue right now. You have a meeting to get to, right? I give and give and you can't offer me a crumb? A maybe? A *chance*?"

"You think I like seeing you holding back, afraid to laugh too loud, keeping to these rooms when you should be able to say and do whatever the hell you please? I hate what I'm doing to you. You never wanted this."

"But if you *loved* me—"

"I *can't* love you! I've upended my world as far as I can. Things are tipping off. *This has to end.*"

She rocked as if buffeted by a hurricane wind. He watched her lips go white with the rest of her. Her fingers twitched at her sides and she swayed again then locked her knees.

*"Bella."* He reached out, feeling the chasm in him widen to a canyon, pushing her further and further beyond him.

She drew a jagged breath and leveled her shoulders. "You should go. I don't want to be blamed for you missing your meeting."

Had that really happened?

One minute she had been feeling sorry for herself over her siblings getting together without her, the next her tiny nascent family of three had been torn down to one and a half.

How had she not fought hard enough? Aside from viewing a few buildings for Maison des

Jumeaux, she had lived as a shut-in again, not wanting to make headlines. As painful as she'd found it when he disappeared for a few days on palace business, she had never once complained. Even his grandmother's frosty behavior at the christening had gone unremarked until today.

All the while, she'd been aware of the days lifting off the calendar like ravens, one by one, swooping away and forming a black, jeering cloud on the horizon. They'd mocked her for loving him despite his lack of commitment. For waiting so patiently for words of love that were never going to come.

Did she regret trying to make their marriage work? No. But failing despite leaving her heart wide open was liable to kill her.

Shaking, she pressed a fresh tissue to her closed eyes, soaking up the leak through her lashes, taking a slow breath and consciously softening her shoulders.

*Uno naranjo, dos naranjos...*

It struck her what she was doing. *Oh, no.*

She pressed the tissue harder into her eyes, becoming aware of the sensations pinging to life in her. A roiling stomach, a creep of foreboding down her spine. Cold specters began to float in her periphery, voicing the ugliest of thoughts. *Why would he want you? You're the broken one. You're soiled.*

"No," she whispered, certain that being susceptible to these attacks *proved* how unworthy she was of love. Was that the ghouls talking? Or the unvarnished truth?

"*Dama*?" Her maid knocked, making her heart leap. Adona entered. "The Private Secretary is here. Her Majesty wishes to see you."

*Not now.* She couldn't. Not with a spell coming on. All of her went rigid while her blood moved like acid in her arteries.

Why did the Queen even want to see her? Her mind raced, trying to think of an excuse, but what could she say?

"Please give me a moment to dress." *Uno naranjo, dos naranjos...*

She chose the dress she'd worn to the christening, since its red and gold were Elazar's national colors and quietly proclaimed her station as the mother of a future monarch. Adona gave her hair a twist while Trella dabbed on light makeup, even though it didn't matter if she put on clown pants or a G-string with water wings. She was going to the guillotine.

As if that were true, the flutters deep in the pit of her belly grew worse. Mario's dour face made his silent escort that much more ominous. Her feet felt like they didn't belong to her. She couldn't make her throat swallow.

The ghouls chuckled as they stuck to her

clammy skin, following her into a stately room of powder blue and white striped wallpaper.

The Queen wore a dark green sweater set and a severe expression. She was seated and Trella was not invited to do so.

Trella ordered her fists to loosen and clasped them in front of her. She took measured breaths, nodded in greeting as the door behind her closed, shutting her in with what she had long suspected was an enemy.

"I'm a woman of well-cultivated patience, but mine has run out," Queen Julia stated. "It would benefit all if you went to Spain for Christmas and did not come back."

Her nails dug into her palm beneath the cover of her other hand. "Xavier suggested the same thing."

Surprise flickered in the Queen's face before she blinked it away. She nodded. "Good. He's finally showing sense."

"I said I'd go if Tyrol came with me." She wanted that so badly, she would buckle into the carpet if the Queen agreed.

The older woman hardened before Trella's eyes. "*No.* But allow me to lend my voice to my grandson's. You do more damage than good by lingering."

The words hit so hard, Trella had to press into her toes to stay on her feet. Still, her inherent streak of bellicosity reared its head. Another woman would have taken this chance to make a good impression and reason with the woman. She wouldn't pour gasoline over the one bridge open to her and light a match.

"Is that what you said to *his* mother when you exiled her?"

The Queen's eyes were so much like Xavier's, it was sheer agony to look into the contempt they held.

"I was told you have a predilection for dramatics." She was like a cat that knew its prey's weakest spots, but took her time piercing them, preferring to terrorize before putting a creature out of its misery. "Xavier's mother has always had access to him. He chose not to pursue a deeper relationship."

"Because you didn't approve of one. Did you? And he couldn't afford to alienate you. He didn't have anyone left." She showed the Queen how she had won more staring contests than she'd lost.

After a moment, the Queen reached very casually to polish her glasses, then perched them back on her nose. "*My* relationship with my grandson is not up for discussion. But if he's asked you to leave, yours with him is clearly over."

*Breathe. Uno naranjo, dos naranjos...*

"Xavier has been conditioned to believe that

people who love him leave and don't come back. I plan to show him that's not true." Would it work? She couldn't think about that right now.

"What he *knows* is that a country can't maintain stability when it's ruled by emotion. Scandal and division among its people are poison. How can he be regarded as a man of integrity when he's with a woman who is nothing but racy headlines?"

"I can't control my headlines!"

"No. You can't. That's why removing yourself is the least you can do. If you care anything for him and your son, protect them."

Score one for the Queen. She knew it, too. She didn't move, but her verbal rapier kept whipping the air, cutting into Trella with casual ease as she spoke again.

"You have no idea the strength required to hold this position. Your weaknesses would become theirs, undermining what has taken five hundred years to build."

"Loving is a weakness?" Where had she heard that before?

The Queen narrowed her eyes. "Your background, your extensive need for therapy and your delicate mental state are weaknesses."

It was as if she saw into Trella's soul where the specters were swirling and cackling, dragging icy fingers over her bones. *She sees you. She knows.*

"The toll of the throne would break someone like you. This is a marathon that lasts a lifetime. What are you going to do when it becomes too much? Retire behind closed doors and burden the palace with making explanations? If that's to be the end result, do it now. Fade into the background before you do any more damage."

"Someone like me," she repeated darkly.

*They won't come for you. They won't want you after this.* It was the oldest, darkest, ugliest voice. The one that made her eyes sting and her heart shrink.

She hadn't come back to her family in pieces because she had passively accepted her situation, though. She had fought with every ounce of will she possessed, from the first moment through all the other struggles to today.

"You know *nothing* about me and what I can endure. Do not confuse my capacity for love as an inability to stand and fight. In fact, love is my *weapon*. You want to go to war with me? Gird your loins. You might rule this country, but I rule the online world. I'm beloved by *billions*. You want to protect what's taken five hundred years to build? I belong to something that's lasted millennia. *Family*. When you die, do you think *duty* will squeeze a single tear from Xavier's eye?"

The Queen went white. "You're becoming hysterical."

"You unleashed this!" She stabbed the air between them. "Love is the only thing that pulls us through hardship. *I know that*. And your tepid love isn't enough to sustain him. Yes, you love him in your stunted way, but you're afraid to show it. Why? Because you might have to deal with grief again? Is that why you don't even look at Tyrol? You're afraid he'll die and you don't want to be attached? Now who's weak?"

Queen Julia gave her bell a resounding shake.

"What's wrong? This is what someone looks like when they're fighting for the people they love. Still think I'm not tough enough for the job?"

"*Get out.*"

"Ms. Sauveterre!" Mario entered. "Please."

She shot him a bitter look on her way past him then ran blindly to her room.

Voices were droning around him, but Xavier wasn't tracking. He was lost in a fog he hadn't experienced since childhood. Twice. The miasma was cold and gray and left him rudderless. His grandmother had been there to lead him along those other two times, but she was the last person he wanted to turn to right now.

Not because he blamed her. No, he blamed himself.

All he could hear was Trella saying, *If you loved me.*

He had said he couldn't love her as if he didn't have the capacity. For a long time, he had believed he didn't. The love he'd once felt for his parents had stagnated under their leaving, stunting him into an inability to feel anything beyond superficial liking.

And yes, Trella had been a distraction lately as they had tried to cram a lifetime into the short marriage they had agreed to, but the fact that their time was finite had put that pressure on them. Hell, he'd called it off and he was still distracted.

*I can live somewhere else.*

The doom he'd felt at that statement couldn't be measured. He tried to picture Patrizia in the room where he'd held Trella and bile rose to the back of his throat.

No, the real problem was that he was afraid to *admit* he loved her. Otherwise, he might feel like this when their marriage ended. But he did feel like this now, which must mean—

"You agree, Your Highness?"

"Pardon?" He sucked in a deep breath, like he was coming out of a coma. What the hell had he done?

"We were discussing where the tax rate should break."

He shook his head, taking in the dozen people slouched over a boardroom table, surrounded by laptops and scratch pads and coffee cups while snow fell beyond the windows.

"Get the Australians on the phone. We'll request an extension into January. We'd rather be with our families through Christmas and I'm sure their people would, too."

*Screw duty.* He had to fix things with the woman he loved.

He rose just as his PA slipped into the room and hurried across with a message that Angelique was trying to reach him.

Frowning, Xavier excused himself and turned on his phone. It lit up with missed calls and texts.

What happened?
Where is she?
Are you with her?

His heart lurched. He hit reply on a video call, moving farther down the hall to an alcove where he had some privacy.

Angelique appeared, her pinched expression deeply anxious. "Are you with her? She keeps texting that she's fine, but she's not fine. I can tell."

"I'm not with her—"

"Damn it, Xavier, you can't leave her alone when she's having an attack!"

Her tone made Xavier's scalp prickle. He only half-believed in the twin connection, but her alarm was genuine enough that he looked for his PA to signal for his car.

"Is there someone who could check on her and get back to us?" Kasim asked.

"She's really scared, Xavier." Angelique sounded half-hysterical herself.

"I'll try her right now. But if you two feed off each other's mood, you should try dialing back your worry and send her some calming thoughts." It came off the top of his head out of frustration and sounded too metaphysical.

Her wet face went blank with surprise. "I honestly never thought of that. God, I'm such an idiot. Of course. I'll text her that I love her."

His conscience twisted as he thought of his own refusal to say those words this morning. He ended the call and tried Trella. She declined to answer, but texted a moment later to say she was napping.

"Everything all right, sir?" his PA approached to ask.

Xavier held up a staying hand as he reached Vincente. "Have you seen Trella today?"

A brief hesitation, then, "Adona said she locked herself in her room after her audience with the Queen."

"She spoke with my grandmother? The car," Xavier snapped at his PA. "Now."

# CHAPTER THIRTEEN

SHE WAS DOING this for Tyrol, she kept telling herself, as she bit down on one of his teethers and counted her oranges. Some women went through the pains of childbirth. Her lot was to weather waves of terror. The irrational, fearful thoughts would pass. The sweating and sobs of insecurity needed to run their course. She just had to breathe and count her oranges and wait it out.

It was easier when someone she loved and trusted sat with her and told her she was safe. She didn't feel safe right now. She felt very temporary and unwanted. Abandoned. Forsaken.

"Shh," she breathed, pushing those thoughts away.

*I am strong. I am loved. I can do this.*

She should have brought her phone in here. All the texting had been breaking her concentration. She had left it on the night table, but now she wished she was reading Gili's comforting words. It was almost as good as having her here.

"Trella!"

Oh, God. What was he doing here? She had locked up and told Adona not to let anyone in. Now he would see her like this and know how cracked she really was.

His footsteps crossed into her bathroom. There was a systematic banging noise. He was opening all the cupboards beneath the dual sinks, looking for her.

"You're sure she didn't leave?"

He had someone with him? And someone who saw him searching cupboards for her? She pulled her feet in tighter, driving the curve of her spine into the wall behind her.

The closet light flicked on, blindingly bright even against her clenched eyes. She made a noise of protest and ducked her head.

"Are you here?" he demanded.

She plucked the teether from her bite. "I don't want you to see me like this."

"Get out and lock the doors."

"Yes, sir." It was Adona and a moment later, a distant noise of a door closing sounded.

Xavier came to the back of the closet and swept aside the gowns. He swore when he found her huddled in the corner on the floor. He crouched and wiped her wet cheek with his hand, drying it on his thigh. "Why didn't you call me?"

"I have to do this alone."

"No, you don't," he said grimly and started to gather her.

"Don't." She pressed as hard as she could into the corner, holding him off with one shaking arm.

"What did she say to you?"

She didn't know if her mental state made him sound that lethal, or if he really was murderous.

"Nothing I don't say to myself." She clenched her eyes in anguish. "I am a detriment. A hindrance. You shouldn't be here. What are you going to do? Run out of every high-level meeting because I'm having an episode? This can't happen. You can't be here. I *have* to do this *alone*."

"Look at me," he said gently.

"No, *you* look at *me*. Is this a queen? It's *not*. I pretended for a while that we could find a way and you followed me through the looking glass because duty chafes and the sex is great, but we knew it couldn't last. You were right, Xavier. This was always going to happen. *This*—" she pointed at her position on the floor "—will happen when I can least afford it. I wish I wasn't this person, but I am. And if you stay in here and nurse me through this, you're only proving that I'm a burden. *I have to do this alone.* I'm an adult who will be a single mother. *I* have to know I can do it."

The mention of living alone sent a tumble of unvoiced fears through her head. Intruders. Kidnappers. A million bad, horrible, terrifying things.

"*Bella,*" he said gently. "I want to talk to you about that. Come on. Come out of here."

"*No.*" She slapped at his reaching hands and said very clearly, "There is no way. None. Just—go look after Tyrol. Please? I can't look after him when I'm like this. If you want to help me, go do that. Please?"

He stared at her, jaw clenched. "I'll bring him to you. Will that help?"

"I can't use him as a crutch. It would turn into me using him all the rest of my life. I won't put that on him. But I'll feel better if I know you're looking after him. Please?" She clutched his wrist. "Will you do that for me?"

"Trella—"

"I'm begging you, Xavier. *Please.*"

He left her in the closet like a child hiding from monsters, hating himself for abandoning her, but she'd knocked the wind out of him. Blind shock held him in stasis for long minutes outside her door.

She thought her attack made her unfit to be his wife?

This was his fault. Not just her breakdown,

but her belief that she had to be perfect to be his queen. She was already perfect in the way of fierce storms and jagged mountains and a flower blooming on a broken stem. Her perfection was in her resilience. That's what was needed in his partner. He loved her for her strength and her ferocious capacity to love and her ability to move forward despite how many times she'd been knocked down.

With her emotional bravery top of mind, he strode to the nursery where Tyrol had just woken.

"I was about to bring him down for a feed—"

"Warm a bottle. I'll take him." He carried his son through the palace, pushing into his grandmother's parlor where she was meeting with Mario.

"Out," he said to Mario, and gave the door a light kick behind the man.

"Your meeting?" his grandmother prompted.

"My wife was indisposed. Someone upset her. I had to care for our son."

"We pay staff to care for him."

"He shouldn't need his parents because you and I didn't? We'll never know, will we?" He set Tyrol in her arms.

"What—"

"Hold him. Feed him."

"What do you think you're proving?" She

lifted her brows and calmly silenced the boy with the nipple.

"What are *you* trying to prove? Look at your great-grandson. Can you honestly say you feel nothing toward him? Because that's certainly how you act."

She looked at the boy. His hand found her thumb and gripped it. A dribble of milk leaked from the corner of his mouth and his eyes were focused on her.

A flinch of anguish crossed her expression before her mouth softened in tenderness. "He looks like your father. Let's hope he doesn't have his temperament. Your father wasn't cut out for the crown. I let him go because I had to, Xavier." Her head came up, blue eyes clouded with sorrow and a pleading for forgiveness. "He wasn't his brother. He wasn't you. He was never going to survive the demands. I let him go and yes, you suffered, but I had already lost both my sons. I couldn't let you go, too."

It was the most sentimental thing he'd ever heard her say. Shaken, he lowered to sit across from her. "I'm a parent now. I do understand," he said at length. "I can't stomach the idea of his being across the city three and a half days a week, let alone not in my life at all."

"You shouldn't have agreed to share him."

"I intend to renege."

Her head came up, surprise in her lined face.

"They're both staying with me. I'm not asking you. I'm telling. If that means you stay on the throne the rest of your natural life, so be it."

"So she's won you over." She sniffed her disdain.

"No, it's up to me to win her."

Her gaze came up again.

"If I can't give the woman I love what she needs, how the hell can I give our country what it needs? She makes me whole. Stronger. I want to be a better man *for her*. That can only make me a better leader. A better king."

Tyrol finished his bottle. She set it aside and brought him to her shoulder to rub his back, exactly as if she'd been mothering infants all these years.

"After the risks she took bringing him into this world, how can you not want to know her? If you knew the things she's been through…" It was killing him, what she was enduring right now, but she seemed to need to prove something to herself and he had to give her that. "She's stronger and more determined than either of us can conceive."

"Her reputation, Xavier. Patrizia is such a good fit."

"I don't love Patrizia. I love Trella." It was conviction. Will. Fate. But he couldn't help

pointing out, "So does everyone else, judging by
the online polls. She's the more popular choice
by a long shot."

"Don't be vulgar," she said crossly. "What
about another baby?"

"We'll find a way. I am going to find a way
to make it work. I have to. I can't live without her."

She let out a sigh of defeat. "Some monarchs
would rather die than watch the next generation
struggle to master the art of ruling. I've always
thought I could give up the throne to you quite
confidently. You rarely make mistakes. I will
trust your judgment holds true in this instance."

He didn't need her approval, but he was glad
to have it. Now he only had to convince Trella
to stay.

Trella woke to bright light beyond the cracks
in her blinds. She squinted gritty eyes at her
clock. It was late morning. She had pumped milk
a few hours ago when her swollen breasts had
woken her, so she wasn't too uncomfortable, but
she missed Tyrol enough that her chest hurt just
thinking about him. She texted the nursery, then
glanced at herself in the bathroom mirror, cring-
ing.

She had done it. She splashed her face, brushed
her teeth, then texted her sister.

*It's over. I'm okay.*

She earned a heart emoji in response.

The residual depression of an attack hovered like a cloud, though, along with profound loss as she accepted she and Xavier would never be. It had been a serious trip to hell and back, but she was *back*. That was something, she reassured herself. She had proved to herself she could not only grit her way through an episode, but that it wouldn't actually kill her.

Where was Tyrol? She checked her phone and saw Gerta had replied.

*The Prince is with the Prince.*

Xavier had had more meetings today. Was Tyrol sick?

She tugged a robe over her nightgown and yanked open her door—to find Xavier slouched in an armchair, clothes rumpled, eyelids heavy. Tyrol was fast asleep on his shoulder. It was such a tender scene, it pushed tears into the backs of her eyes.

"Is he okay?" She gently gathered the sleeping baby into her arms.

"Missing you, but otherwise fine. He just ate. That's purely for show," he added as Tyrol began to stir and fuss at the sound of her voice.

She sat to feed him, but Xavier was right.
Tyrol nodded off before he'd taken more than a
few gulps and she cuddled him instead. Oh, he
smelled good and his skin was so soft. His hair
was fine against her lips and his grip on her finger, endearing.

*I'll always come back to you, my sweet, sweet
boy.* She had thought about him a lot last night.
She had thought about Xavier and how delusional she had been, ever thinking she could be
his queen when she had this awful shortcoming.

Fresh agony washed over her.

When she couldn't avoid it any longer, she
looked at where Xavier hadn't moved.

"Was it a rough night?" she asked.

"For him? Not particularly. For me? Yes."

With a lurch in her heart, she noticed the glass
on the table beside him. "Are you hungover?"

"No. I poured it, then thought I'd prefer to be
sober if you decided you needed me."

"Were you worried? I'm sorry."

He snorted and reached for the glass. "Now,
she's sorry." He made a face at his first sip and
clunked the glass back onto the table. "Mostly
water now. How was your night?"

"Awful."

He nodded in grim agreement.

"Why are you angry? Xavier—"

"I'm not angry." He shot to his feet, though,

and paced a few steps only to turn back abruptly. "I am angry. I respected your wishes because fine, I accept that you had to feel you could get through an attack alone. But I have issues, too. *Because* of you. You ignored my texts for months before you admitted you were pregnant. Then you locked me out of a delivery room while you *flatlined*. We've been apart more than we've been together. You damned well need to stay accessible to me. I need to know you're alive, even if you're not at your best."

That was the problem. Sometimes she was at her absolute *worst*.

And she really wasn't up for a scolding over it. Or facing how she was supposed to be accessible from across the city. Much as she had given his grandmother a show of bravado, that's all it had been. She couldn't be his wife. She knew that now and it hurt so badly; she had to escape to hide how anguished she was.

"I want to shower. Can you take him and order breakfast?"

He said nothing as she handed him Tyrol again.

Swallowing, heavy with a melancholy that would never lift, she went back to her room and started the shower, blinking hot eyes as she did. She wasn't ready. If she hadn't had that stupid attack, if they hadn't had that big fight yesterday, they could still play alternate universe a few more days. Why had she shortchanged them like that?

She stepped under the spray and turned to see Xavier had come in behind her.

"Where's Tyrol?"

"Nursery." He peeled off his clothes, dropping them to the floor as the glass walls gathered steam.

"What are you doing?"

"What does it look like?" He opened the door and came in, crowding beneath the head that rained from the ceiling.

They'd showered together before, daily, but that was *before*.

"Xavier, I can't." Her heart was too tender, still pulling at all its old fractured lines and itching from fresh stitches.

"What did I just say about locking me out?" He cupped her wet head and planted a single kiss on her mouth, hot and possessive. Oddly tender.

She moaned and ducked her face as soon as he let her, tucking her forehead into his collarbone. Her vision filled with the golden skin she loved, taut and smooth over hard muscles. He was growing aroused, which always excited her.

"You know we're just putting off the inevitable. You were right all along," she muttered.

"You're staying here. We're staying married."

For a couple of heartbeats, she thought she'd imagined it, then she jerked back her head and looked at his implacable expression. The wetness in her clenched eyes wasn't from the water raining on her face.

"The future king decrees it? We both know I'm not a suitable queen."

"You are."

"You saw me last night!"

"And I see you this morning, having survived it. That's who and what you are, *bella*. You survive. You push through hardship to come out the other side, bruised maybe, but you make it. You don't give up on yourself, you would never give up on Tyrol and I won't let you give up on us."

Her mouth trembled. "If you loved me—"

He made a noise of imprecation. "If? *If*?" His hands cupped her face again. "You put a spell on me the first time we met. You gave me a son and helped me kick-start my heart so I could give him the love he deserves. Of course I love you, you infernal woman. How the hell else are we here?"

"You don't have to yell about it. What about Patrizia?"

"Are you seriously worried about a woman you have never met? You've ruined her life, *bella*. Just as you have ruined mine. But you won't feel bad about it because you've saved us both from a terrible mistake."

"Tyrol did. Lay the blame where it belongs."

"I thought I just did. God, I love you." He kissed her and this time he meant it, fusing his mouth to hers and letting her taste his desperation.

She grasped his wrists and pulled away, gasping, trying to speak from soul to soul. "Do you mean it? Because I don't think you understand how much it means to me that you can accept me, with all my breaks and imperfections. Don't say it unless it's true."

"You are flawed. You're unpredictable and defiant and shameless. You're also brave and creative and you love with everything in you. If you can rise out of your past and risk your heart, what kind of coward would I be if I refused to do the same? I'm privileged to be one of the people you love, Trella. I know what an exclusive club it is."

They kissed again and this time they didn't stop. The water rained down, washing away any ghosts that lingered, leaving only the love they had for each other.

Her body melted against his and she found herself pressed into the wall by his flexing muscles.

"Mine," he growled, kissing and licking at her

neck and shoulders, across her breasts then between them. "There is no more locking yourself away. Understand? Not from me." The kisses continued, down her arms, across her hips.

She needed this doting attention. This all-consuming passion from him. It soothed and healed and made her feel cherished. By the time he knelt and hitched her thigh onto his shoulder, she was nearly weeping at the sweetness of him pouring such love all over her.

Her stomach jumped in reaction at the way he claimed her. He pleasured her until she was delirious, crying out with abandon. Then he stood and took her where she was, against the hard tiles, naked and slick as he drove into her, hard and deep. It was lust and bonding and naked unabashed love. When the climax came, they were in it together, trying to meld their slippery bodies into one being so they could never be separated again.

Then they leaned there, panting and wrung out, the water cooling, barely able to find the strength to get to the bed. They fell asleep in each other's arms, waking to make love again without the frantic pace driving them.

"We have time, *bella*. All our lives," he murmured, rocking lazily within her.

She released a shaken sigh, combing her fingers through his hair and was astonished at the lightness in her. The breadth of view. Years and years to come of this.

"I love you. You're the only man who could have given me this."

"You're the only woman I want or need. The only woman I could love so much."

Later that evening, he placed his rings on her finger as they dressed for dinner. The Queen wasn't one for making apologies, either, but she invited them to dine with her and suggested Xavier take his son and wife to Spain the day after Christmas if it was something Trella wanted.

It was, he did and it was wonderful.

EPILOGUE

*Press release five years later...*

*Inconceivable Twins!*

The Deunoro Palace surprised the world today by announcing that King Xavier and Queen Trella are celebrating the arrival of their daughter, Vivien.

Queen Trella's sister, Queen Angelique of Zhamair, also celebrates with her husband King Kasim the arrival of their third child, and first daughter, Genevieve.

While it was widely reported that Queen Angelique was carrying twins, it has now been revealed that, with the help of the world-renowned fertility clinic in Lirona, Queen Angelique was implanted with one egg from each set of parents.

Mother and babies are in excellent health.

The Queens' brothers, Henri and Ramon

Sauveterre, were on hand with their own growing families to welcome this latest and most unusual pair of Sauveterre twins.

\* \* \* \* \*

*If you enjoyed*
*PRINCE'S SON OF SCANDAL*
*why not explore the first three parts of*
*Dani Collins's*
**THE SAUVETERRE SIBLINGS** *quartet?*

*PURSUED BY THE DESERT PRINCE*
*HIS MISTRESS WITH TWO SECRETS*
*BOUND BY THE MILLIONAIRE'S RING*

*Available now!*

# Get 2 Free Books,
## Plus 2 Free Gifts—
### just for trying the Reader Service!

# Get 2 Free Books,
## Plus 2 Free Gifts -
### just for trying the *Reader Service!*

# Get 2 Free Books,
## Plus 2 Free Gifts—
### just for trying the Reader Service!